The Valentine's Day Disaster

by Brandi Dougherty

Scholastic Inc.
New York Toronto London Auckland Sydney
Mexico City New Delhi Hong Kong Buenos Aires

ISBN-13: 978-0-545-03168-4
ISBN-10: 0-545-03168-0

Text copyright © 2008 by Brandi Dougherty

12 11 10 9 8 7 6 5 4 3 2 1   8 9 10 11 12 13/0

Printed in the U.S.A.
First printing, January 2008
Book design by Jennifer Rinaldi Windau

So many people
made this book possible
by believing that it was,
especially my family.
Thank you!
-B.D.

CHAPTER 1
The Disaster

"All in favor raise your hand."

Maddy Wilkes sat on her hands and glared around the classroom at the other student council members. The hand of every person in the room was high in the air, except for two: Maddy's of course, which was trapped under her leg, and her best friend Sarah Warren's, which wavered somewhere between her shoulder and her side.

"Well, I guess that finally settles it then," said Jessica Saunders, eighth-grader and student council president. "The Valentine's Day Dance will be held next Friday, February 16th. We'll meet again on Monday to form committees and make the final plans for delivering heart-o-grams on Valentine's Day. We've got a lot of work to do since we had so much trouble voting on a date, so we'll all need to pitch in to get everything done. Thanks, guys, see you Monday!"

The front door of Evergreen Middle School burst open.

"This is totally, completely, and absolutely unfair!" Maddy shouted as she stormed down the sidewalk in her Adidas sneakers, snow catching the bottom of her jeans.

"Maddy, wait up! Don't walk so fast. You know I can't keep up in these boots!" Sarah called after her, dodging an icy patch in her pointy black boots.

Sarah and Maddy had been BFFs since third grade, when Sarah's family had moved to Hamilton. They liked to joke that their last names were responsible for their friendship. The girls had always been assigned seats next to each other in elementary school. Sometimes the "W" seemed to be all they had in common, but they were still great friends.

"I can't believe they picked next Friday for the Valentine's Dance. I mean, Valentine's Day will be over by then, anyway!" Maddy yelled back to Sarah.

"But I thought you didn't even like Valentine's Day," said Sarah as she caught up. "Why do you even care?" she asked distractedly. She was busy unbuttoning her long, black wool coat so she could straighten her skirt and cable-knit tights.

Maddy stood and waited with her mitten-clad hands folded over the front of her white puffy down jacket.

"You're right, Sarah, I don't like Valentine's Day. In fact, I hate Valentine's Day! After what happened last year I will never eat chocolate shaped like a heart ever again. And I will never wear anything pink again. And I will definitely not be sending any valentines. Or any cards at all. Ever again in the *entire* month of February. No way." Maddy's bright blue eyes stared intently at Sarah. "It's a good thing your birthday isn't in February or we'd have to celebrate it in March!" Then she turned on her heel, tossed the end of her green knit scarf over her shoulder, and continued to stomp her way home.

"So if you still hate Valentine's Day, then what's the problem?" Sarah asked, determined to keep up.

"The problem is that my soccer league fund-raiser was supposed to be in the gym on Friday night. But now, because of the stupid dance, we get bumped to the library. It was going to be so cool in the gym. We had an auction planned for the stage. There were going to be food tables and music on the basketball court. Now it will be too cramped and boring and no one will even come. How are we going to raise enough money to go to the state tournament this spring?" Maddy seemed close to crying, but the look on her face was pure frustration.

"Can't you change the date of the soccer fund-raiser?" asked Sarah, trying to be helpful. "And you're not still mad about what happened last year, are you? I mean, no one really remembers . . ."

"No one *remembers*?!" Maddy's temper flared. "No one remembers the total embarrassment I faced in front of the entire lunchroom? No one remembers Glen Plimpton telling everyone he loved me? On a *microphone*, Sarah, in the cafeteria on Valentine's Day?" she fumed. "No one *remembers* calling me Mrs.

Plimpton for the rest of the year and making kissy noises every time Glen and I were in the same room together?"

"Yeah, I guess I remember it pretty well," said Sarah, trying not to laugh.

"Gee, thanks!" Maddy growled.

"Oh, come on, Maddy, don't be mad. You know Glen only did that because Kyle Lester dared him to." Sarah patted Maddy's shoulder with her light pink cashmere glove. "Glen would do anything Kyle asked him to. He was dying to be the class clown, like Kyle. I think he still wants to be, actually."

"He's a clown alright. His red curly hair looks just like a clown wig." Maddy almost half-smiled at her own description.

"I mean, it wouldn't have been so bad if my sister hadn't heard about it. You should have seen her. She was so excited that I had been humiliated in front of the entire school. She was the one who started the whole 'Mrs. Plimpton' thing, you know. And her hot-shot friends thought it was perfect."

"Really?" asked Sarah. "I didn't think Monica was that mean. I thought band-geek Glen started that himself."

"Nope. That was my lovely sister. She'll do anything to torture me. I bet everyone would have forgotten about it if Monica hadn't been there to remind them all year long!"

The girls rounded the corner onto Third Street and could see the pink, sparkly door of Sugar Hill Bakery from half a block away. Maddy's mom was part owner and the head baker at Sugar Hill — the most popular bakery in town.

"Ugh. Look at the bakery," Maddy muttered, pushing a few light brown curls back under her striped wool hat. The windows were covered with pink hearts, red cupids, and shimmering silver streamers. Inside, the girls could see puffy white papier-mâché hearts hanging from every inch of the ceiling.

"I'd bet you a million dollars my mom did all that herself."

"I think it looks cute!" said Sarah.

"This is just the beginning. Do you have any idea how ridiculous my house gets on Valentine's Day?" continued Maddy, ignoring Sarah's comment. "My mom runs around in a total frenzy taping hearts to anything that will stand still. And the whole time she's singing gushy, sappy love songs and blowing kisses to my dad. It's so disgusting."

"That doesn't sound so bad . . ." Sarah stared intently at the ground like she was looking for something she had dropped.

"Well, it's not just that," mumbled Maddy, embarrassed that she had forgotten about Sarah's parents' divorce. It had been almost two years already, but it was still hard for Sarah and her younger brother Jack, who was only seven. Sarah and Jack saw their dad on some weekends and holidays, but he was so busy with work that even those times often got bumped. Maddy knew that had been happening more and more lately.

"You should see my sister," Maddy went on, hoping Sarah would stop thinking about her parents. "Monica gets so many balloons and teddy bears and pink flowers and chocolates from boys, she can't even get them all home."

"That doesn't sound so bad, either. I wouldn't mind getting pink flowers or chocolate from a boy. I mean, pink *does* go great with my dark hair," Sarah said, running her gloved hand down her perfectly straight, long brown hair.

"Well, it's . . ." Maddy started to say.

"Hey, Sarah! Hey, Mrs. Plimpton!" Monica yelled out the door of Sugar Hill. Monica was fourteen (exactly eighteen months older than Maddy) and in eighth grade at Evergreen Middle School. She was one of the most popular girls in the whole school. The fact that she had a younger sister at the same school who she could embarrass on a daily basis definitely helped her status (or at least *she* liked to think so). Monica loved holidays just as much as Mrs. Wilkes, so she always helped out at the bakery during busy times of the year. Valentine's Day was one of the busiest and Monica's favorite.

"What's going on, dorks?" Monica asked as she wiped her hands along the bottom of her pink apron with the words "I'm Sweet" written in glitter across the front.

Maddy pushed passed her into the bakery. "Nothing. Where's Mom?" she asked sharply.

"She's in the back designing the most beautiful wedding cake. The couple who ordered it is getting married on Valentine's Day. Isn't that the sweetest thing *ever*?" Monica gushed, holding her hand to her chest.

"How swe . . ." started Sarah.

"How gross," finished Maddy.

"Girls! How was school?" Mrs. Wilkes emerged from the kitchen looking like she'd been in a food fight. Bits of pink frosting clung to her wild brown hair. Flour and sugar streaked her cheeks and arms. Her apron and Sugar Hill T-shirt underneath were splattered with chocolate batter.

"Want a cookie?" she asked, as she tried wiping chocolate from her eyebrow.

"Can I have mine with black frosting?" Maddy responded. She was dying to get out of the bakery before anything pink or heart-shaped came near her.

"Oh, Maddy, you're so silly," laughed Mrs. Wilkes.

"She thinks I'm kidding," Maddy whispered to Sarah. Maddy's mom always thought Maddy was joking around about things that Maddy actually took very seriously.

"Here you are, girls. Aren't these cookies just adorable?" Mrs. Wilkes remarked as she handed Sarah and Maddy two giant, heart-shaped sugar cookies exploding with pink frosting and tiny red candy hearts. "They're our signature cookie this year."

"Thanks, Mrs. Wilkes. I love them!" Sarah responded enthusiastically. Maddy narrowed her eyes at Sarah and Sarah shrugged, taking a big bite of her cookie.

"Anything exciting happen at school today?" Mrs. Wilkes asked.

"More like something tragic," Maddy responded.

"So, Mrs. Plimpton, when is *your* wedding?" Monica interrupted with a smirk.

Maddy turned to see her standing in the kitchen doorway holding up miniature statues of a bride and groom.

"Shut up, Monica!" Maddy snapped.

Monica disappeared into the kitchen again and Maddy turned back to her mom, ready to tell her the bad news about her soccer fund-raiser. But Mrs. Wilkes was crouched underneath the counter sifting through a box and mumbling to herself about plastic cupids.

"So, Mom, listen to this." Maddy set down her cookie so she could tell the story better. But Monica flung open the kitchen door again. This time she had a white dishtowel on her blond head and she was carrying a bouquet of plastic flowers. She started marching toward the front of the store like a bride, singing, *"Maddy and Glen forever."*

Maddy stiffened and reached for her backpack. "Come on, Sarah, let's go."

"Thanks again for the cookie, Mrs. Wilkes," Sarah shouted as Maddy pushed her out the door.

Mrs. Wilkes peered over the counter and looked confused. "Of course, dear," she replied.

"Bye, Mom, see you at home." Maddy let the pink door slam behind them, glitter falling like snow. She continued to stomp along the sidewalk as Sarah tiptoed behind her.

"Oooo, she just makes me so mad!" Maddy shouted, balling her hands into fists. Her face was beginning to get red. "I can't stand my sister and the way she still teases me about Glen Plimpton! And all this Valentine's Day stuff — it's driving me crazy!"

"Maddy . . ." Sarah started between bites of her cookie.

"It's time to get serious about this," Maddy continued, ignoring Sarah again. "I've had enough of Valentine's Day and I'm not going to let this dance ruin my soccer fund-raiser! And I'm definitely not going to let my sister keep torturing me about Glen. We need a plan . . . an anti-V-Day plan."

"V-Day? That's what you're calling it now?"

"Yeah. V-Day."

"Don't you think you're taking this a little far?" Sarah looked concerned. Maddy was getting so upset!

"Sarah, I have to figure out how to save the fund-raiser. And if I don't put an end to all this V-Day stuff with my sister she's never going to stop. She can't keep treating me like this!"

The two girls had reached the park on Dogwood Avenue. Maddy lived with her parents, Monica, and their dog Pete at one end of Dogwood, at 121. Sarah lived with her mom, Jack, and their two cats Sugar and Spice at the other, at 760. The street was divided into two sections by a large park and playground. That had always been Sarah and Maddy's meeting spot. They walked to school every morning and home again on days that Maddy didn't have soccer practice. They had their routine down pat and didn't even have to talk about it — they just knew.

"So, do you want to come over and help me with my anti-V-Day plan?" Maddy asked hopefully.

"Uh, I can't. I have to watch Jack until my mom gets home. Plus I'm working on this new skirt pattern and I really want to get started sewing." Sarah loved fashion and had taken a sewing class over the summer. Her mom bought her a sewing machine for Christmas and she was starting to get really good at making clothes. She had created a couple of patterns already and had even made a simple T-shirt for Maddy.

"We'll have plenty of time to work on it tomorrow night," said Maddy. "You're still staying over, right?"

"Yeah, we can, um, talk about it then, I guess," Sarah responded quickly. "See you tomorrow, Maddy."

"Bye, Sarah. Remember, anti-V-Day!" Maddy called out, raising her fist in the air.

She watched Sarah wobble as she tried to squeeze between two enormous snowbanks in her fancy boots. She let out a small laugh and shook her head. *I don't know how Sarah walks in those things,* Maddy thought.

As Maddy turned toward 121, she thought about how to make her anti-V-Day plan work.

CHAPTER 2
The Soccer Game

Maddy always woke up early on Saturdays. She loved the idea of having a whole day to do whatever she wanted, and Monday still felt miles away. And Saturday morning at this time of year almost always meant a soccer game. Weekday soccer practice during the winter was mostly just short warm-ups and kicking the ball around, but the weekend meant full, indoor games against other teams in the city league. Maddy loved playing soccer. She loved the intensity of running up and down the field. She loved the suspense of penalty kicks. She loved it all. She could feel the energy of the competition and the challenge start to warm her up inside. She leaped out of bed and pulled on her soccer shorts and league T-shirt and headed downstairs for breakfast. The smell of waffles was already wafting toward her bedroom door.

"There you are, Madeleine." Maddy's mom was

standing in the hallway ready to call up the stairs. As usual, she had food all over her — waffle batter this time.

"I never have to call you down for breakfast when I'm making waffles. I thought something was wrong."

"Nope. Just getting ready for my game. I have to prepare myself mentally, too, Mom," Maddy replied.

"That-a-girl, Mad." Maddy's dad poked his head out into the hall. He was the only person allowed to call her 'Mad.' "It's always good to do a little mental preparation before a game — keeps you focused and sharp."

Maddy's dad was the assistant coach of Maddy's soccer team. Maddy liked having her dad for a coach, most of the time. It was great to be able to talk about all the plays and games with him and he was super enthusiastic about Maddy's team. Sometimes, though, he could be embarrassing.

"Well, let's eat before it gets cold," Maddy's mom said as she ushered Maddy into the kitchen and then turned back to the hall to call Monica, who always needed to be called down.

"Are you all set for the game, Mad?" Maddy's dad asked between sips of coffee.

"Yep, I'm ready." Maddy filled a glass with orange juice. "I'm anxious to try out my new move . . ."

"Ugh, soccer talk already." Monica appeared at the kitchen door wearing flannel pajama pants, fuzzy pink slippers, and a huge Hamilton High sweatshirt. Her perfect shade of blond hair was piled on top of her head and secured with a giant rhinestone-covered clip.

"Good morning, sweetheart," said Mr. Wilkes.

"Morning, Daddy," Monica replied in her sugar-coated 'princess' voice (as Maddy liked to call it).

"So, anyway, Dad," Maddy continued. "My new move is this . . ."

"Maddy, can we please talk about something other than soccer on a Saturday morning?" Monica sighed into her juice glass. "I mean, for once, *puhleease*," she added, just to be extra dramatic.

"Oh, I'm sorry. What would *you* like to talk about, Princess Monica?" Maddy snapped.

"Anything but that!" Monica snapped back.

"Alright, girls," Maddy's mom interrupted. "Why don't we just enjoy our breakfast in silence if you're going to start arguing on a perfectly nice Saturday morning?"

Both girls scowled silently at their waffles and started to eat. Like Maddy, Monica was rather opinionated and outspoken, and because they were so close in age, they didn't get along too well. Every once in a while they'd manage to laugh and be silly like they did when they were younger, but mostly Monica was all about boys and being popular — two things Maddy had no interest in at all.

"John, did you see that article about the new development plans downtown?" Maddy's mom asked her dad. "Do you think your company will get a bid?"

"I sure hope so," Mr. Wilkes replied. "We've put in for it, so keep your fingers crossed."

Maddy's dad worked for a big construction

company in Hamilton. Most of the year he was the foreman on construction jobs and worked a lot of hours, but during soccer season he usually requested a slower schedule so he could make it to most of Maddy's games and practices. Maddy loved that he took extra time off from work to spend with her. She knew it was a big deal, but she also knew how much her dad liked coaching.

Maddy took a huge bite of waffle and made a face at Monica. Monica put a strawberry in her mouth, covering her teeth completely, and smiled back. They actually started laughing at each other and tried to see who could make the grossest face.

"Well," said Maddy's mom, shaking her head. "I guess that's better than arguing."

Monica wiped the strawberry juice from her face and reached for a waffle. "So, Maddy, who are you going with to the Valentine's Day Dance? Glen? Maybe he'll bring his oboe and serenade you."

"Oh, did they finally decide when the dance will be held?" Mrs. Wilkes asked excitedly.

"Yep, it's Friday night!" Monica replied. "I can't wait. I wonder how I'm going to decide who to go with? And Mom, I *have* to go to the mall this weekend. I have, like, nothing to wear."

"Maddy, isn't your soccer fund-raiser Friday night?" Maddy's dad asked.

"Yes, Dad, exactly." Maddy put down her fork. "Now it's a huge mess and no one's going to come, and . . ."

"Maybe that wrap dress I saw last week is still on sale," Monica continued.

"That was cute," Mrs. Wilkes nodded.

Maddy jumped to her feet, almost knocking over her dad's coffee. "Why does everything have to be about stupid Valentine's Day? My soccer fund-raiser is a complete disaster and all you can talk about are clothes at the mall?" Maddy fumed, her blue eyes fixed angrily on the surprised faces of her family.

"Chill out, Maddy!" Monica reacted. "Not everything's about soccer, either, you know."

Maddy started to say something in response to Monica, but thought better of it. She sat back down

and tried to finish her breakfast as quickly as possible.
The rest of the family ate a little more slowly and
carefully, as if they were afraid Maddy might explode
again. She got up, rinsed her plate, and put it in
the sink.

"Dad," Maddy tried to take a calming breath. "I'll
be in the truck."

Maddy waited in the truck for what seemed like an
eternity before Monica and Mr. Wilkes came out.
Maddy knew that Monica was taking as long as she
possibly could to get dressed for gymnastics practice,
just to annoy her even more. She had taken gymnastics
since she was old enough to walk, and much to
Maddy's dismay, she was amazing at it. She also
planned on being a cheerleader at Hamilton High next
year and everyone knew that meant one thing: instant
high-school popularity.

Monica and Maddy both stared silently out the
window as they drove to the Evergreen Middle School

gym. Monica jumped out as soon as the truck stopped in the parking lot. "Thanks, Daddy. I'll get a ride home with Marisol," she said sweetly to Mr. Wilkes. Then she stuck her tongue out at Maddy and strutted off toward the door to the gymnastics floor. Maddy glared back and then followed her dad in the opposite direction to the indoor soccer fields.

"Just focus on the game, Mad." Mr. Wilkes patted Maddy's back as they reached the door.

"I will. Sorry for freaking out at breakfast this morning, Dad."

"That's OK. I know your sister can be a little hard to handle sometimes. Just don't let it get to you right now. And don't think about the fund-raiser during the game. We'll figure something out."

Maddy nodded and hurried to join her teammates, who were warming up across the field.

"Hey, Emma, hey, Li," Maddy said as she ran up. She focused on her stretches and tried to put Monica out of her mind. She waited until Michele arrived before breaking the news about the fund-raiser.

"So, guess what, guys."

"What?" they asked, practically in unison.

"I want you all to know I did everything I could," Maddy put her hands out cautiously to prepare them for the news. "But, the student council voted to hold the Valentine's Day Dance next Friday night."

"Oooo! Really?" Emma squeaked excitedly. "Oh, my gosh, that's so soon! What am I going to wear?"

"Wait, what?" Maddy was confused. "No, Emma, you don't get it — our soccer fund-raiser is next Friday. Now it's going to be held in the library. But no one is even going to come if the dance is that night!"

"Oh, that is bad," said Michele. "What are we going to do?"

"Well, I'm working on this plan — this anti-Valentine's Day plan. And I think if we can get enough people involved to boycott the dance, everyone will realize how dumb it is and they'll decide to come to our fund-raiser instead," Maddy said in a rush of energy.

"Anti-Valentine's Day? Are you serious?" Li asked.

"Of course I'm serious, Li. This is serious business! We *have* to have our fund-raiser or we can't go to State."

"But why can't we just move the fund-raiser to another weekend so we can all go to the dance?" Emma chimed in.

"Yeah! Perfect!" the other girls added.

Maddy shook her head. "The gym is booked for months in advance, that's why they had to bump our fund-raiser to add the dance. There's no way we can get another weekend before the spring tournament."

"Well . . ." started Li.

"OK, girls, it's game time," Coach Simmons shouted from across the field. Everyone jumped up and ran to do a huddle with the coaches.

"Yeah, OK, we can, um, talk about this after the game!" Maddy called after them, but no one seemed to hear.

Final score: Smith Street Towing: 2; Hollister, Adams, and Lewis, Attorneys-at-Law: 1. Maddy and the rest of the Hollister team shuffled toward the sideline after giving their "good game" handshakes to Smith Street.

"I totally thought we had that," Maddy said, readjusting her messy ponytail. "If I hadn't missed that goal, we would have at least tied."

"I'm the one who let them score so easily, Maddy!" Li replied, shoving her goalie jersey into her backpack.

"Girls, you played a great game. Don't get down on yourselves — we'll work on some mechanics next week."

"Thanks, Mr. Wilkes," called Emma. "Bye, Maddy, see you Monday!"

"Wait, Emma, we have to talk about the dance!" Maddy shouted after her, but Emma was already pushing open the door.

"Maddy, I'm going to talk to Coach Simmons for a minute, let me know when you're ready," Mr. Wilkes said.

"OK, Dad, I just need to get my stuff together and talk to the team about something," Maddy said, as she bent down to untie her cleats and put her Adidases back on. When she stood up the gym was practically empty. *How did everyone get out of here so fast?* she wondered. Maddy grabbed her bag and started walking reluctantly toward the bleachers where her dad and Coach Simmons were chatting.

"Hey, Maddy, how's it going?"

Maddy spun around to see Josh Martin jogging her way — his sandy blond hair hanging in his eyes as usual. Josh had transferred to Evergreen from another middle school halfway through last year and they had gone to the same soccer camp last summer. Though Josh was a little quiet, they got along great and had plenty to talk about, both being huge soccer fans. This year they had English class together and sat next to each other, so they had gotten to know each other a little better. Now they saw each other at soccer practice and games on the weekend, so they would talk there, too.

"Hey, Josh. It's going OK, except for totally losing that game just now."

"That sucks — I thought for sure you guys would beat Smith Street."

"Yeah, tell me about it. How was your game?"

"Good, we beat Mr. Anderson's team three to nothing." Mr. Anderson was their English teacher.

"Way to go," Maddy replied quietly.

Maddy knew that Josh was the best soccer player in the entire seventh grade, maybe even in all of Hamilton.

"What's wrong?" asked Josh, brushing aside his hair.

"Well, besides losing the game, I found out on Friday that the girls' soccer fund-raiser got bumped from the gym for the Valentine's Day Dance."

"Really? How can they do that?" Josh asked, seeming genuinely upset.

"I guess student council can do whatever they want since they control the gym schedule. I totally voted against it, but no one was on my side," Maddy sighed.

"I'm sorry, Maddy. That's lame. What are you going to do?" Josh asked.

"Well, I'm trying to work something out. I kind of have a plan but I'm not sure yet," Maddy said. She wasn't ready to tell Josh her anti-V-Day plan. She still had to work out the details.

"Well, I'll definitely try to think of something," Josh offered.

"Thanks, that's nice of you," Maddy answered.

"OK, cool. So, I'll see you on Monday, I guess."

"Yep, see you Monday."

Maddy picked up her stuff again and walked over to her dad. Josh lingered for a second watching Maddy cross the gym. He gave a little sigh and ran back toward the boys' team.

CHAPTER 3

The Fight

That evening Maddy sat cross-legged in the middle of her bed with her laptop propped on a light green pillow in front of her. Maddy's favorite color was green, so her room was made up of various shades of it. She had a forest green duvet cover on her comforter with lighter green sheets and pillows. She also had an alternate set of green-and-yellow striped sheets that she loved. Soccer posters, game flyers, and photographs covered her walls. She had a bulletin board above her desk with a few pictures of her soccer team friends on it, but most of the space was taken up by pictures of her and Sarah. She had photos from each year that they had been friends. Her favorite was a Halloween photo from fourth grade: Sarah was an alien princess and Maddy was a giant soccer ball. Tacked up around the photos were various tickets, concert programs, and postcards from places she and Sarah had been and fun things they had done.

Maddy started up her computer and opened a new document. She began to type slowly as she thought of what to say.

"Ladies and gentlemen of the Evergreen Student Council," Maddy said out loud as she clicked on the keyboard. "No, that's too formal and weird."

There was a tiny knock on her bedroom door and Sarah peeked in.

"Hey, Sarah, come in! I didn't think you'd get here till later."

"Yeah, dinner with my dad was kind of short. He had to get back to work," Sarah said softly.

"On a Saturday night?"

"I guess so," she replied as she took off her black wool coat and gloves. She was wearing dark blue jeans and a red velvet blazer with a black T-shirt underneath and black flats. She had silver hoop earrings with tiny red and black glass beads hanging from them and a matching red-and-black beaded bracelet. Sarah's outfits were always perfectly accessorized.

"So," said Maddy, sensing that Sarah didn't really want to talk about dinner, and anxious to get to her plan, anyway. "I've been thinking about the anti-V-Day plan. What if we write a really dramatic speech and I deliver it at the student council meeting on Monday? Everyone will demand a re-vote and the dance will be canceled!" Maddy said triumphantly. "Here's what I have so far: Ladies and gentle . . ."

"Um, can we work on that later, Maddy?" Sarah interrupted. "I was hoping we could talk a little school gossip first and paint our toenails. I brought pink for me and black for you," Sarah said hopefully, holding up a little pink bag covered in marabou.

"Oh, alright . . . I guess."

Maddy closed her laptop and scooted onto the floor next to her bed.

"So, did you see Jessica Saunders on Friday? She was wearing that new brand of jeans that costs like five thousand dollars. Well, not really that much, but they're super expensive!" Sarah said as she arranged her pedicure supplies on Maddy's desk chair.

Maddy wanted to focus on her speech, not on her toenails, and not on what Jessica Saunders was wearing. But she felt bad about Sarah's dinner with her dad, and she didn't want to be insensitive.

"I didn't notice her jeans, but I did see that none of the boys in student council were even paying attention to what she said. She could have been talking about going to school all year long and they wouldn't have cared!"

"Totally!" added Sarah.

It was rare for Maddy to gossip about clothes and boys and school stuff, so Sarah was happy to keep it going. Sarah wished Maddy was as into those things as she was. She liked hearing about Maddy's soccer games and everything, but sometimes all she wanted to talk about was a new clothing trend or a designer she'd read about and Maddy didn't really follow that stuff.

"So what do you think of our English class this year?" Sarah asked.

"It's so much better than last year!" Maddy responded.

"I know!"

"Mr. Anderson is such a great teacher and we have so much more time for writing. . . ."

"No, Maddy, I meant about the *boys* in our English class," Sarah laughed, shaking her head.

"Oh, right. Um, Josh Martin is really nice," said Maddy as she tried to apply black polish to her big toe.

"Really?" asked Sarah with a sly smile on her face.

Maddy was too focused on polishing her toe and not the carpet to notice Sarah's look.

"Yeah, he's just so . . . interesting," replied Maddy. "He's kind of quiet when you first talk to him. Even though he's been at Evergreen since last spring, I feel like no one knows that much about him."

"I know he won that art thing last year," said Sarah, her brown eyes staring at Maddy in disbelief. Maddy *never* talked about boys.

"Yeah, he beat Michael Moriarty, too," answered Maddy. "I mean, he was an eighth-grader. And he had won every year. No one could believe that Josh Martin, a new sixth-grader, even stood a chance. Plus he plays soccer and my dad told me the boys' soccer coach said he's the best player in the league," Maddy continued.

"You totally like him," Sarah blurted out. "I've never heard you talk about a boy like this. And I've seen you talking to him in class. You *like* Josh Martin!"

"What?" Maddy gasped. "Are you kidding me? I do *not* like Josh Martin. I just think he's nice *and* he's a good soccer player. We're friends. That's all."

"Uh-huh," Sarah replied.

Maddy put the polish down on her desk chair. "Can we please talk about the anti-V-Day speech now?"

Sarah continued applying pink to her toes in perfect strokes. "I think he's friends with Kyle Lester."

"You mean Kyle Jester?" Maddy asked, smiling. "Did you hear Mr. Anderson call him that last week? It's so perfect."

"Well, he *is* really funny and he has that cute little dimple on his cheek when he smiles." Sarah looked up from her toes. "I have to tell you something, Maddy, but you can't tell anyone."

"What?" Maddy asked, unsure what important thing Sarah was about to say.

"I kind of have a crush on Kyle . . . a big crush."

"Are you serious?" Maddy was totally surprised. Kyle was loud and obnoxious in class and Sarah was so quiet.

"Yeah, I mean he's so cute and his jokes are really funny," Sarah added. "Don't you think?"

"I guess so, but Kyle Jester? Really?"

Maddy's bedroom door flew open and in bounced Monica, wearing black leggings, a denim mini, three different tank tops layered together, and a hooded sweater.

"What's going on, girls?" she asked as she jumped onto Maddy's bed and grabbed a pillow for her lap.

"I like your outfit, Monica," Sarah responded, scooting over to give Monica more room.

"Thanks! I just got this little sweater hoodie for my birthday. Isn't it the cutest?"

"Totally," said Sarah.

Monica picked up Sarah's polish. "So, who's this Kyle kid?" she asked with a grin. "Oooo, I love 'Sweet Dreams,' it's the perfect shade of pink — not too bright and not too orangey, you know?"

Maddy couldn't believe she'd been listening outside the door. "Don't you have somewhere else to be?" she asked impatiently.

"I'm waiting for Jessica's mom to pick me up, so I've got a couple of minutes."

"Jessica Saunders's mom?" Sarah asked, wide-eyed.

"Yeah. Now who's Kyle?"

"Um, he's this boy in our English class and he's so funny," Sarah said, pulling her feet up to blow on her toes. "He has the cutest dimple . . ."

"Monica, Sarah and I are discussing some important business right now and it would be great if you would GET OUT!" Maddy shouted. She hated the idea of Sarah talking to Monica about anything.

"What's *your* problem?" Monica asked. "I just want to hear about Sarah's crush."

"My problem is you! We were actually talking about my anti-V-Day speech at student council and we would appreciate it if you would leave us alone." Monica looked confused. "Anti-V-Day? What does that mean?"

"It means anti-Valentine's Day. We're planning to boycott the Valentine's Dance," Maddy responded, crossing her arms.

"Boycott the Valentine's Dance? Why in the world would you want to do that?" Monica looked from Maddy to Sarah for an answer, but Sarah just shrugged. Maddy noticed Sarah's response and started to get frustrated. "Because we don't care about the stupid Valentine's Day Dance! We don't care about getting flowers and candy from dumb boys! We have better things to do. Like raise money for soccer and . . ." Maddy was out of breath.

"Mom is going to freak when she finds out about this, Maddy. You know how she feels about Valentine's Day. And personally, I think you're the only one who cares about soccer. It's soooo boring!" Monica added as she stood up and adjusted her outfit.

"GET. OUT!" Maddy screamed at the top of her lungs.

"Geez, you don't have to be a brat, I'm just saying. Well, have fun with your lame little speech, girls." Monica darted out the door before Maddy could scream again.

Maddy got up and slammed the door behind her.

"Why does she have to be my sister?" she said through gritted teeth. "Why couldn't she be some foreign exchange student leaving at the end of the school year? Or some girl my parents took in for a couple of weeks while her mom was in the hospital or something? I can't stand her."

"She's not that bad, Maddy," Sarah said. She would never admit it to Maddy, but she would do anything to hang out with Monica and her friends sometimes. They were just so cool and seemed so much older. All the girls wanted to be their friends and all the boys had huge crushes on them.

"Whatever. Let's get to work on this speech." Maddy walked over to her desk to retrieve her laptop.

"Can't we just watch a movie or something? I don't really feel like working on a speech right now," Sarah asked in a small voice. She was tired of Maddy getting so worked up about Monica and she couldn't figure out how to tell her she thought the whole anti-V-Day thing was kind of silly. Sarah was dying to talk more about Kyle and the possibility of going to the dance with him, but she knew Maddy would get even more annoyed.

"Fine," Maddy responded with a huge sigh. "We'll just work on it tomorrow. At least we have one more day before school."

Maddy and Sarah barely spoke after the movie credits rolled. They turned off the TV in the living room, walked single-file up the stairs, brushed their teeth, and went to bed. The next morning Maddy woke up early. She hadn't slept very well and was still upset about the night before. She quietly turned on her laptop and started working on the speech before Sarah was even awake.

"What are you doing?" Sarah asked half an hour later as she removed her sleep mask.

"Just working on my speech," Maddy mumbled.

"Oh," Sarah quietly groaned. "Well, I actually have to get home. My mom wants me to watch Jack again for a little bit," she said more loudly.

Maddy gave Sarah a look. She knew Sarah wasn't telling the truth; she just didn't want to help Maddy with the speech.

"Fine. Bye, then," Maddy said and then instantly felt bad for being mean. But not bad enough to stop Sarah from leaving. Sarah sighed, got up, and grabbed her bag and coat from the floor. She went into the bathroom to change.

A few minutes later Maddy could hear her shoes clicking on the stairs and the squeak of the front door as it closed. Maddy slumped onto the bed on her stomach. Why was everything turning into such a disaster? She just didn't understand what the big deal was about Valentine's Day. All she wanted was for her fund-raiser to be OK. And for Monica to stop teasing and embarrassing her so much. And for things with Sarah to go back to normal. Why did it seem like Sarah only wanted to gossip and talk about boys lately? They used to have so many other things to talk about.

Maddy spent most of the afternoon working on her speech. She took a few breaks to do her English homework and go online, but that was it. Maddy's mom took Monica and her friends to the mall and asked if Maddy wanted to go, but there was no way she was going to participate in that trip. Maddy's dad even offered to kick the soccer ball around in the snowy backyard for a while, but she just didn't feel like it. All she could think about was saving the soccer fund-raiser and her fight with Sarah.

At dinner that night Maddy silently pushed her mashed potatoes around on her plate like she was shoveling snow. Maddy's mom talked about how busy the bakery was and how many Valentine's Day orders they had so far. Maddy's dad talked about the construction project downtown and how big it was going to be. Then her parents talked about a new car they had seen one of the neighbors driving. Monica seemed pretty quiet, too, not really adding anything to her parents' conversation, until:

"Have you heard about Maddy's speech, Mom?" she asked, trying to sound casual.

Mrs. Wilkes turned toward Maddy and put her fork down. "No. Are you giving a speech, Madeleine?"

"She sure is," interrupted Monica. "She's calling it 'Anti-V-Day' and she wants the student council to cancel the Valentine's Day Dance on Friday." Satisfied, Monica sat back in her chair and pushed her straight blond hair away from her shoulder. She couldn't wait to see her mom's reaction.

"What? Maddy, why?" Her mom looked genuinely worried. "Why are you so upset about Valentine's Day? It's such a lovely holiday. Your father and I met on Valentine's Day, you know," she added, winking at Maddy's dad.

Maddy took a deep breath and put down her fork, too. "I know, Mom. I just don't think it's fair that my fund-raiser got bumped for a silly dance. And I'm sick of everything pink and frilly and . . ."

"She's just worried Glen Plimpton might not ask her," Monica interjected.

"Oh, is that the sweet boy that liked you so much last year?" Mrs. Wilkes cooed. "That was just the cutest thing when he . . ."

"Mom, please!" Maddy said. "It wasn't cute, it was embarrassing! How would you feel if some dorky boy you didn't even know that well told the entire school he liked you?"

"Oh, honey, I wasn't trying to tease, I just thought it was sweet," Mrs. Wilkes responded.

"I'm serious, Mom, you have no idea what it was like!" Maddy slapped her hand against the table. "There I was, minding my own business, eating lunch with Sarah like always, and all of a sudden this geeky band nerd is standing in the middle of the cafeteria holding a microphone and telling the entire school that he loves me! Before I knew what was happening, everyone was pointing and laughing and teasing me! I've never been more embarrassed in my life."

Maddy sighed. It didn't seem like anyone else at the table understood how horrible it had been. "Can I go to my room now?" she asked, hoping to escape clearing the table this one time.

"Madeleine, honey, don't get so upset." Mrs. Wilkes tried to sound soothing.

"I just want to forget about it," Maddy sighed again.

"Yes, Mad, you can go," Maddy's dad said finally.

Maddy sat on her bed with her laptop resting on her legs. She fought back tears as she opened her journal. Maddy wrote in her journal almost every day. She loved writing almost as much as she loved soccer. If she wasn't a professional soccer player when she grew up, she was pretty sure she'd be a journalist. She started to type about her fight with Sarah and how much Monica was annoying her, but it was just making her feel worse. Why was everything such a mess?

She closed her journal and opened the speech. She read through it and made a few more changes. *I don't know if this is going to work*, she thought. Then Maddy logged in to her chat program to see if Sarah was online. She thought for sure she'd be ready to apologize for what had happened, but she wasn't logged in. Maddy minimized her soccer ball chat icon at the bottom of her screen and opened the soccer league Web site. She was responsible for updating the girls' league page with all the game information and stats. She added the results of the weekend's games and started to write a blurb about an article she had read in *World Soccer Magazine* when her chat icon popped up in front of her. It was a message from Josh.

kickart: hey maddy
mad4soccer: hi josh
kickart: still thinking about how 2 help w the fund-raiser . . . any new ideas?
mad4soccer: kind of . . . not sure it will work tho.
kickart: did u finish yr eng homework?

mad4soccer: yeah . . . u?

kickart: yeah, it was pretty easy . . .

Maddy stared at her screen having no idea what else to write.

kickart: well . . . just wanted 2 say hi & c if u had a plan 4 the fund-raiser yet

mad4soccer: hi. yeah, i'll let u know

kickart: k. see u 2mro

mad4soccer: k bye.

Maddy was annoyed she didn't think of something more interesting to say. Then she thought about Sarah accusing her of liking Josh.

"We're just friends," she said out loud to herself as she shut down her computer and turned off the lamp next to her bed.

CHAPTER 4

The Speech

On Monday morning, Maddy lingered at the park. She didn't know if she should wait for Sarah to walk to school or not. They'd never been in a fight that had lasted more than a day. Maddy didn't know how to handle it. She shifted back and forth in her puffy down jacket and green scarf. She had jeans and Adidas on, as usual, and her favorite T-shirt under a brown V-neck sweater. She always felt most comfortable in jeans — they were practically her uniform. Maddy sighed and decided to start walking. Sarah wasn't usually late, so she probably didn't want to walk together.

As Maddy headed quickly to school, she thought about her fight with Sarah. She felt like Sarah should apologize for storming out of her house without saying anything. But she knew she had been mean, too. She just didn't understand why Sarah wouldn't support her anti-V-Day plan. Isn't that what BFFs did? Supported you no matter what? Maddy had stood up for Sarah in the fifth grade when Rachel Allenberg was bullying her. That's just how it worked: If your BFF was in trouble, you came to the rescue.

🧁 🧁 🧁 🧁 🧁 🧁

After homeroom, as Maddy walked down the hall, she could hear everyone discussing the Valentine's Day Dance. Not only that, but there were already several posters announcing the dance being hung on the walls. She was surrounded by it. A huge group of girls was huddled around a locker struggling to get a peek at a skirt in a magazine that one of the girls wanted for the dance.

"Isn't it perfect?" the girl screeched. "Now I just have to figure out how to get Justin to ask me!"

Maddy had to move out of the way of a bunch of eighth-grade boys who joked and shoved one another as they talked about who they would ask to the dance.

"Dude, you should ask Clarissa!" one shouted as he pushed his friend hard in the shoulder.

"No, *you* should ask her, dude. I'm asking Eva," the other boy responded with a jab to the stomach.

Maddy couldn't believe the dance was all anyone could talk about. She reached into the pocket of her jeans and felt the crumpled paper her speech was typed on. Her hand got a little sweaty as she squeezed it.

This is a bigger problem than I thought, Maddy realized as she turned the corner and entered her English class. *I better get this anti-V-Day plan going before it's too late.*

With a minute left before the bell, Maddy decided to approach Mr. Anderson about her plan. He was not only a coach for one of the boys' soccer teams, but he was her favorite teacher and a writer, too — just like Maddy.

"Good morning, Mr. A."

"Morning, Maddy," Mr. Anderson responded without looking up from what he was reading.

"So, Mr. A, I have this problem that I wanted to talk to you about. It's about the Valentine's Day Dance on Friday," Maddy started.

"Can't help you there, Maddy," Mr. Anderson interrupted. "I was pretty awkward in middle school. I don't even think I went to my Valentine's Day Dance in seventh grade," he chuckled.

"No, no, that's not what I mean," Maddy stammered. She was totally unprepared for what Mr. Anderson had just said. "I'm talking about the soccer fund . . ."

The final bell drowned out Maddy's words.

"Well, that's the bell. Maddy, take your seat, please."

She scowled at Mr. Anderson, but he continued to read from his book. Maddy was mortified that he thought she wanted dating advice for the dance. He hadn't even listened to her! She slunk to her seat and flopped down in her chair, sighing hard. Josh turned around and looked at Maddy.

"Rough morning?" he asked.

Maddy looked up confused. She had forgotten for a moment that Josh sat right in front of her.

"Um, yeah, kind of, I guess."

"What's the matter?"

"I'm starting to think that my whole anti-dance thing might not work out."

"Hmmm," Josh said thoughtfully. "Well, maybe a meteor will crash into the school on Friday and only damage the gym. Then everyone would have to come to the fund-raiser!" he said with a smile.

Maddy laughed. "I guess there's always that."

From two rows back and to the left, Sarah stared at Maddy and Josh. *Maddy totally likes him*, Sarah thought. *I can't believe she won't admit it.* Just then, Sarah felt a tiny wad of paper stick in her bangs. She fished it out and looked around the room. Kyle was laughing hysterically. She gave him a huge smile and a little giggle, tossing it back in his direction.

"Nice shot," she said, still smiling. "I just saw that happen on TV the other night." Sarah was glad she had decided to wear her navy blue cashmere sweater that day. She had paired it with a brown corduroy skirt that matched her eyes perfectly. She also wore dark blue tights, brown flat boots, and a thick navy headband that made her dark hair look great.

Maddy heard Sarah's voice and turned in her chair. Sarah was focused intently on Kyle and twirled a piece of hair around her finger while she spoke. Maddy had only seen Sarah act this way one other time and that was around Monica's friend Lacey's older brother, so it didn't really count. She definitely had a crush on Kyle.

"Me, too!" Kyle said excitedly. "Wasn't that the funniest thing ever? That's what made me think of doing it, but I didn't think it would work."

Sarah started to respond, but was cut off by Glen Plimpton's high-pitched, super loud voice. Glen planted his bright red head directly between Sarah and Kyle. Sarah's smile quickly faded.

"Hey, guys, whaddaya talkin' about? Did I miss something? I heard you laughing and it seemed like I might have missed a joke or something." Glen was talking so fast Sarah could hardly understand him.

"We were just talking about this show we saw on TV, that's all," Kyle responded, trying to be nice, but hoping Glen would go away.

"Oh, well, I saw this show on the Animal Channel last week where this snake swallowed a bird whole. It was so cool and you could see the shape of the bird . . ."

"Thanks for that disgusting imagery, Glen," Mr. Anderson interjected, walking toward the front of the room. "Now, how about taking your seat so we can talk a little literature here?"

"Uh, OK, sure, Mr. A."

Kyle and Sarah exchanged a smile and Kyle pretended to throw the wad of paper at Glen. Maddy turned back toward the front of the room and Josh quickly dropped a piece of paper on her desk. It was a drawing of a meteor crashing into the gym. Josh had drawn several students running from the gym saying, "I guess we better go to that soccer fund-raiser!" and "Good idea! Let's go!" Maddy let out a small laugh and covered her mouth, hoping Mr. A. wouldn't ask what was so funny. Josh grinned and turned back to the front of the room.

Maddy tried to focus on what Mr. Anderson was saying, but all she could think about was giving her speech at the student council meeting later. She was starting to feel really anxious about it. Josh's drawing had definitely helped calm her nerves a little bit, though — it was just what she needed.

As everyone filed into the student council room that afternoon, Maddy started getting nervous again. Really nervous. She was worried about how everyone would react, but she was determined to go through with it.

If I can squash this dance, Maddy thought, *maybe Monica will take me more seriously and stop being such a jerk all the time.*

"OK, everybody, let's get started," Jessica called from the podium. "We have a lot to do. We have to assign committees for the heart-o-grams and the dance."

"Uh, Jessica, just a sec." Maddy raised her hand. "I have a speech I'd like to give first."

Jessica wrinkled her forehead and glanced at her watch. "Um, I guess so, as long as it's short," she added, moving to the side of the podium. Maddy slowly walked to the front of the room and pulled the crumpled paper from her jeans pocket. She cleared her throat and unfolded the paper, smoothing it out on the podium.

"Fellow student council members," she began, her voice cracking a little. "As some of you may remember, the girls' soccer league fund-raiser is also scheduled to take place on Friday night." Maddy looked up from her sweaty paper and scanned the room briefly. She saw two boys passing a football back and forth near the windows, one girl at the back of the room trying to blow the biggest bubble gum bubble humanly possible, and several people near the front yawning and doodling in their notebooks. She tried to straighten up and talk a little louder, but she also felt her knees start to shake. "If the soccer fund-raiser is held in the library instead of the gym, as originally planned," Maddy pointed a finger in the air for emphasis, "then the girls' soccer team will NOT raise enough money to be able to go to the state soccer tournament this spring. A tournament," she continued, "that showcases the best soccer talents this state has to offer."

As Maddy finished her passionate plea to save the fund-raiser and cancel the dance, she looked again at the sea of faces in front of her. She saw the same bored looks as before as well as a few new worried ones. She also noticed several students (including Sarah) who were trying desperately to look busy doing something else just to avoid eye contact with Maddy.

"So that's why I think we should have a re-vote on the dance," Maddy added, slapping her hand against the podium in a final burst of energy.

Jessica stood up and straightened her fitted pink turtleneck over her black skirt. She gave Maddy a sweet smile and patted her on the shoulder like she was a two-year-old.

"OK, everyone. Apparently Maddy wants a re-vote on the dance. So, all *still* in favor of holding the Valentine's Day Dance on Friday night *and* in the gym, raise your hand."

Maddy jerked her head toward the crowd expecting to see maybe one or two hands in the air. But every hand was in the air. A couple of girls put both hands in the air. Maddy spotted several boys near the door who had their hands in the air and they didn't even belong to student council — they just snuck in to stare at Jessica. And to top it all off, Sarah's hand was in the air.

"Happy, Maddy?" Jessica smirked, gently pushing Maddy aside and taking her place in front of the podium again.

"So anyway, let's get down to business."

As Maddy shuffled back to her chair she could feel her cheeks getting hot and tears welling up in her eyes. She wanted to run out of the room, but decided that would draw even more attention and she was determined to hold her ground. Sarah glanced in Maddy's direction, but didn't dare make eye contact. She was too embarrassed.

Jessica quickly started calling out the names of various dance committees: ticket sellers, refreshments, advertising, clean-up. . . . Maddy kept her arms folded and a scowl on her face the whole time. There was no way she was getting stuck on a dance committee.

"Last committee is the decorating committee," Jessica said twenty minutes later. "Who would like to join?"

Out of the corner of her eye, Maddy saw Sarah's hand dart into the air once again.

"Sarah Warren, OK, Lizzie Bronstein, Abby Colton, Ben West, Francine Holland, OK. Who else? Nissa Long and Mary Wu. OK, great."

Maddy glared hard at Sarah, trying to get her to look up, but Sarah's eyes remained glued on the desk in front of her. *How could she do this to me?* Maddy was astonished. *How could she betray me like this?*

"OK, so everybody needs to make plans with the other members in their committee. Let me know if you have any questions. We'll have another committees-only meeting on Thursday to make sure everything's set. Thanks, guys!" Jessica shouted cheerfully.

The minute Jessica stepped away from the podium, Sarah jumped up, grabbed her bag, and ran out of the room.

"Sarah, wait!" Maddy called after her, struggling to get her stuff together through the blur of tears in her eyes.

Maddy ran out into the hall and straight into Monica and two of her gymnastics friends. They were waiting for Jessica outside the student council room.

"Whoa, there, Mrs. Plimpton! Where are you headed in such a hurry?" Monica asked as loudly as she could. She put her hand out so Maddy couldn't get by.

"Ha! I totally forgot about that whole Glen Plimpton thing," Monica's friend Emily laughed. "That was classic."

"If you're looking for your boyfriend, Maddy, I would suggest the geek-squad chairs in the band room," added Marisol, Monica's other friend. Just then Jessica strutted out into the hall.

"Hello, ladies, what's going on?" said Jessica.

"We're just trying to help Maddy find her boyfriend Glen Plimpton," said Marisol.

Jessica put her hand on her hip. "Did Glen put you up to giving that speech?" she sneered at Maddy.

"Maddy, you didn't actually give that stupid speech, did you? I'm *so* embarrassed that you're my sister," Monica groaned, slapping her hand to her forehead.

"Why do you guys have to be such jerks?" Maddy yelled. She pulled away from Monica and her friends and started down the hall, again fighting back tears.

"You're going the wrong way, Maddy, the band room's that way," Marisol called after her.

CHAPTER 5

Another Fight

Maddy ran down the hall toward the front entrance of the school. She checked near Sarah's locker and by the cafeteria, but there was no sign of her. Just as she was about to give up and walk home, she spotted Sarah at the end of the hall talking to some of the other girls on the decorating committee.

As she approached the group, Maddy heard Sarah say, "So we'll talk online tonight and then meet again tomorrow to brainstorm. And I'll find out from Jessica what our budget is."

Wow, Maddy thought. *Sarah's usually so quiet in groups, but it sounds like she's in charge of the committee.*

"Sarah, can I talk to you for a sec?" Maddy asked.

"Um, sure," Sarah responded. "So I'll talk to you guys later?" she asked, and then turned toward Maddy. The girls opened the front door of the school and started walking home.

"I can't believe you did that to me!" Maddy exclaimed as soon as they were outside.

"What!? Did *what* to you exactly?" Sarah responded, her face turning beet-red almost instantly.

"I can't believe you not only totally ignored me in there, but you didn't even stand up for me when I was giving my speech! *And* you actually volunteered for one of the dance committees! You know how important this was to me, Sarah!"

"How important sabotaging the dance was?" Sarah yelled back at Maddy. "I happen to *want* to go to the dance. And so does most of the rest of Evergreen Middle School, if you hadn't noticed! I'm sorry about your soccer thing, Maddy, I am, but I think you're being a baby about this." Maddy stopped and stared at Sarah in disbelief.

"I am *not* being a baby. I just want everything to be the way it was. I want our soccer league to raise the money we need for State, I want my sister to leave me alone, and I want us to be BFFs again. It seems like all you want to do lately is talk about boys and clothes and *now* the Valentine's Dance!"

Sarah sighed and started walking again. "It just seems like you never want to do fun things anymore. Why *can't* we talk about crushes and what to wear to the dance instead of writing a student council speech on a Saturday night?

"I mean, I saw you talking to Josh in class this morning," Sarah continued. "It totally seems like you like him. Why can't you just admit it?"

Maddy felt exhausted. After giving her speech and dealing with all the taunting from Monica and her friends, she had no energy left. And now, all of a sudden, she and Sarah were in an even bigger fight and Sarah had to bring up Josh again.

"I don't like Josh! Why does everyone have to give me such a hard time?"

"Come on, Maddy . . ."

"I'm not kidding! We're just friends. Just leave me alone, OK?" Maddy turned so Sarah wouldn't see the tears that were now streaming down her cheeks. She straightened her backpack on her back and started to run down the snowy sidewalk. She just wanted to get away from everything that had happened today.

Sarah watched Maddy run for a minute and looked down at her outfit. *I could probably catch her in these boots, but I don't even want to!* Sarah thought. Her shoulders slumped a little and she kept walking toward Dogwood.

🧁 🧁 🧁 🧁 🧁 🧁

Maddy opened the front door and dropped her backpack on a chair in the hallway. The family's yellow lab, Pete, appeared from the kitchen and ran to greet her.

"Peetie! At least someone still loves me, huh?" she said as she buried her face in Pete's warm fur and tried not to cry again.

"Maddy, is that you?" her mom called from the kitchen.

"Yeah, it's me."

"Come and tell me about your day."

Maddy was hoping she could just sneak up to her room and try to forget about her day, but something in the kitchen did smell good. She took off her snowy Adidases and her puffy coat and put them next to her backpack.

Maddy pushed the kitchen door open and was greeted by what looked like a commercial for Valentine's Day. There were treats and pastries everywhere, in every shade of pink imaginable: cupcakes, sugar cookies, heart-shaped cheesecakes, and mini strawberry tarts.

Maddy shielded her eyes. "Geez, Mom, what is going on?"

"Hi, honey! We've had so many orders for Valentine's Day this year that Gloria is baking at the bakery and I'm baking here — we needed more kitchen space! Isn't it crazy?"

"Yes, that's exactly what I was going to say," Maddy remarked, turning back toward the door.

"Stay and have some hot chocolate, Maddy, I want to hear about your day," said Mrs. Wilkes.

Maddy could never pass up hot chocolate. It was her favorite. "OK, maybe for a minute." Mrs. Wilkes handed Maddy a steaming mug of hot chocolate with a giant homemade marshmallow floating on the top. Maddy pulled a stool up to the counter where her mom was working and let out a huge breath as she sat down.

"Is something wrong, sweetie?" Mrs. Wilkes asked in her usual, slightly distracted manner. She was trying to get just the right color of pink for her next batch of frosting and didn't seem to notice that red food coloring had started dripping down her hand and onto the floor. But Pete had noticed and was there to catch every drop.

"I think I just had the worst day of my life," Maddy replied, letting her head fall onto the arm of her sweater.

"Oh, Maddy, it can't be that bad, can it?"

"Well, first of all, I gave that speech in student council about canceling the Valentine's Day Dance."

Mrs. Wilkes opened her mouth to speak.

"I know, Mom, I know." Maddy held up her hand. "Then Monica and her stuck-up friends started teasing me about Glen Plimpton again. Then Sarah and I got into a huge fight on the way home. She didn't even stand up for me at student council, Mom." As Maddy used her finger to push the marshmallow around in her cup, she noticed Pete run from the kitchen, but she didn't think much of it. She was feeling too miserable to care what Pete's problem was.

"I'm sorry you had a fight with Sarah, honey. Friends don't always do what we think they should."

"And then she started accusing me of having a crush on Josh Martin and not telling her about it. I mean, Josh and I are friends from soccer camp and now we have English class together, but that's it!" Maddy continued.

"Well then, you should just explain that to her," Mrs. Wilkes offered.

"I tried, Mom. I feel like no one listens to what I'm saying."

"Honey, I think you get a little too worked up sometimes. Maybe you need to think about what happened from Sarah's point of view, too."

Maddy could feel a small, tense sensation in the pit of her stomach. Deep down she knew her mom was right — she did get worked up about things. But her dad said she was just really passionate about stuff!

"Yeah, maybe," she said quietly.

"So what did the other student council members decide about your speech?" Mrs. Wilkes asked, trying not to seem too interested.

"They all thought I was crazy and voted to keep the dance."

"Oh!" Maddy's mom said a little too excitedly. "Well, I mean it's probably something that some of the kids are really looking forward to. . . ."

"Yeah, I'm starting to get that. I'm just worried about soccer, that's all."

"I know, Maddy, but you'll figure it out. You always do."

"Thanks, Mom." Maddy got up from her stool and grabbed her mug. "And thanks for the hot chocolate."

"Of course, sweetie, any time."

Maddy stopped in the hall to get her backpack. She headed up the stairs thinking about what her mom had said. As she passed Monica's room, she realized she could hear her laughing and talking on the phone.

That's weird, Maddy thought, *I didn't hear her come home.*

Maddy closed her bedroom door, set her hot chocolate on the nightstand, and sunk onto her bed. *How did everything turn into such a disaster?* she thought. *Just a couple of days ago things were fine, and now they're a total mess. Maybe Mom's right. Maybe I do need to think about how Sarah feels. But it doesn't really seem like she's thinking about how I feel! This is really important to me!*

Maddy had a ton of math homework to do, but couldn't bring herself to face it. She felt so bad about her day that she knew she couldn't concentrate on

schoolwork yet. She rummaged around in her desk
and brought out some drawing supplies. She spread
them out on the floor in front of her. First she picked
up a fat pink marker and drew a big heart on a piece of
poster board. After she filled in the heart, she traced a
large circle around it with a black marker. Next she
drew a wide black line diagonally across the center of
the heart. At the top of the page in bright purple
marker she wrote: "This dog supports the Anti-V-Day
cause!" She figured even if no one else was on her side,
she could convince Pete to be.

Maddy felt a little better after making the sign. She
opened her journal on her laptop and tried to write
about the day, but with each sentence she started
sinking back into her bad mood.

She decided to go downstairs and watch TV until it
was time to set the table for dinner. Hopefully that
would take her mind off things. *I'll just do my math
homework later*, she reasoned.

Maddy flipped through the channels distractedly,
trying to find something even remotely normal to

watch. *Click*, a soap opera; *click*, a cooking show: "How to Win Over Your Sweetie with this Valentine's Day Feast"; *click*, a dating show; *click*, an old Looney Tunes cartoon featuring Pepé Le Peu.

"Geez," Maddy said. "Is *everything* about stinkin' Valentine's Day?" She clicked the remote again and found a show on the Animal Channel that filmed a snake swallowing a bird whole.

"That's better," she said, setting down the remote.

"Gross! Maddy, turn the channel!" Monica appeared from behind the couch in her slippers.

"No. It's educational."

"No, it's not. It's gross. Change it!"

"No."

"Mommmm!" Monica screamed.

Mrs. Wilkes entered the room holding a spatula and a mixing bowl. It looked like there was more batter on her apron than in the bowl.

"What?"

"Maddy won't change the channel and this show is disgusting."

"Monica, Maddy was watching TV first . . . ick, that *is* gross. But she was watching first, give her a break. Come and help me finish this batch of cupcakes. We need to start dinner soon, anyway."

"Fine." Monica marched out after Mrs. Wilkes. "Happy?" she sneered back at Maddy.

"Yup," Maddy responded with a smile. She sunk back into the couch to watch her show.

A few minutes later, Maddy's dad arrived home from work. He came into the living room and sat on the edge of the recliner. Maddy thought he looked tired.

"Hey, Dad," she said, trying not to sound too down.

"Hiya, Mad, how was your day?" he asked.

"Pretty much terrible. How was yours?"

"Yeah, about the same, I think. We lost the bid on that construction job downtown." Mr. Wilkes grunted as he pulled off his work boots.

Maddy watched her dad intently. She knew that would have been an important job and would have meant a lot of money for his company.

"I'm sorry, Dad," she said.

"It's OK. We'll get another one. So what was so awful about your day?"

"Oh, nothing really . . . you know, just middle-school stuff." Nothing that had happened to Maddy today seemed very important right now.

"Well, hang in there. I'm going to go clean up before dinner." Mr. Wilkes patted Maddy's head as he left the room.

Maddy clicked off the TV and bravely headed toward the kitchen to help set the table.

At dinner she managed to avoid being teased by Monica. The girls ate quietly while Maddy's parents talked about the lost bid. Even Monica knew now wasn't the time for joking around. After dinner, Maddy cleared the table like she normally did and then helped her dad with the dishes. She felt like helping out a little more than usual.

Then Maddy went up to her room to start her math homework, but got online instead. Maddy and Sarah always IM'ed on Monday nights to make plans for the week and to chat about homework. They had a system for everything and it was being totally disrupted by the fight. She could see that Sarah was logged in and chatting, but she wasn't IM'ing Maddy.

She's probably IM'ing those other girls on the decorating committee, Maddy thought. *There's no way I'm going to IM first. She should apologize to* me. She stayed online much later than she should have, looking at the state soccer tournament Web page, checking the latest pro soccer stats, and hoping Sarah would IM and apologize about the fight, but she never did.

"Maddy, get off that computer and go to bed!" Mrs. Wilkes called from the hallway.

"OK, OK!" Maddy responded, closing her web browser.

Oh no, my math homework! Maddy remembered as she got up to brush her teeth. *Oh well, I'm sure it's not that big of a deal, just this once . . .*

CHAPTER 6

The Fund-raiser

Tuesday morning was like any other school morning in Hamilton, except for two things. Maddy had walked to school alone for the second day in a row and she felt a heavy sense of dread hanging over her. Dread that the next day was Valentine's Day. Dread that the dance and the fund-raiser were both four days away *and* dread that she and her best friend were in the worst fight they'd ever had. As Maddy sat in homeroom waiting for the bell to ring, she noticed a couple of fellow student council members whispering and gesturing toward her. In the hall on the way to English class, she saw two eighth-grade girls from the meeting giving her weird looks.

Great, she thought, *now everyone thinks I'm totally nuts.*

Sarah was already sitting at her desk when Maddy entered their English classroom. She watched Sarah as she made her way to her desk, hoping Sarah would glance up and give her an apologetic look. She didn't. Her gaze was fixed on the back of Kyle Lester's head. And his gaze was fixed on a comic book he was trying to read and hide at the same time. And Glen Plimpton's gaze was also fixed on Kyle as he struggled to read the name of the comic book so he could write it down.

Maddy slid into her seat as the bell rang and Josh turned to give a quick wave and a smile.

Well, at least someone doesn't think I'm crazy . . . yet, she thought.

"So," Josh started. "There's something I wanted to ask you."

"Yeah?" Maddy was curious.

"Good morning, my fine feathered students," Mr. Anderson boomed from the front of the class. "I don't suppose anyone's interested in attending an English class this morning? Kyle? Josh? Maddy? How about it?"

Josh turned reluctantly in his seat and Kyle stashed his comic book.

"Let's begin where we left off yesterday in chapter six of our anthology, shall we?" Mr. Anderson continued.

Maddy opened her book and flipped to a clean page in her notebook. She tried to pay attention, but her mind was swimming with thoughts about Sarah and their fight. And what had Josh wanted to ask her?

The rest of the morning passed a little more smoothly. Maddy only got a few more strange looks from student council members and she started to think maybe the drama about her speech was starting to disappear. But a whole new drama arrived with math class. Ms. Jenkins surprised the class with a pop quiz and Maddy knew she did terribly on it.

Of course, the one time I don't do my math homework, we get a pop quiz. This is just great, she thought. She slumped down in her chair and felt like sliding right under her desk. *Maybe if I focus really hard I can create some sort of portal and disappear completely.*

"Alright, class, let's grade the pop quiz together," Ms. Jenkins called from her desk.

Since Maddy's portal trick hadn't worked and she was still sitting in her math class chair at 11:38 on Tuesday, she had at least hoped to avoid her grade until the next class. No such luck. And it was just as bad as she had feared — a D. Maddy just stared at the paper. The grade looked foreign to her. She couldn't remember getting a D on anything. *Ever*.

On her way out after class, Ms. Jenkins stopped her.

"Madeleine, do you have a minute?" she asked.

"I was, um, on my way to lunch, but . . ."

"This will only take a second."

"OK," Maddy responded quietly, letting her backpack fall onto her feet.

"I just saw your score from the pop quiz, Madeleine. Not so hot. Is everything OK?"

Maddy's face started to get red. "Yeah, I'm fine. Just wasn't ready for it, I guess," she stammered.

"Well, this score isn't like you. I know you can do better. If this happens again, we'll need to have a little chat. OK?" Ms. Jenkins said.

"Yeah, OK."

The lunchroom was full and buzzing by the time Maddy arrived with her lunch tray. She looked toward the table in the center of the room that she and Sarah usually shared, but it was empty except for two sixth-grade boys. She scanned the cafeteria and found Sarah seated at a back corner table usually reserved for eighth-graders. She was laughing and talking to several girls from the decorating committee, and yes, some of them were eighth-graders. She and Maddy locked eyes for a split second. *Is Sarah wearing eye make-up?* Maddy wondered, straining to see Sarah's face again, but Sarah had already turned away.

Maddy's gaze continued across the lunchroom until she found Emma, Li, and Michele from her soccer team. Relieved, Maddy hurried toward an empty chair at their table.

"Hey, guys, mind if I join you?"

"Sure, Maddy . . . where's Sarah?" Li asked.

"Oh, she had a meeting or something," Maddy responded quickly. She didn't want to answer questions about their fight or draw attention to the fact that Sarah was eating with eighth-graders directly across the room.

Just then Josh and two boys from his soccer team wandered up.

"Hey, Maddy. It's packed in here. Can we sit at your table?"

"Yeah, OK, sure," said Maddy, a little surprised.

"This is Emma and Li, and you know Michele from English. This is Josh."

"Hi."

"And this is Matt and Toby," Josh said, gesturing toward his friends.

"Aren't you in my math class?" Toby asked Maddy.

"Yeah, how'd you do on that pop quiz?" she asked.

"Not great. That was pretty brutal," Toby responded.

Josh grabbed the seat next to Maddy and started unwrapping his turkey sandwich.

"So any luck on your plan against the dance?" Josh asked her.

"Ugh, no. I tried to get the student council to vote against it yesterday, but it was a total disaster," Maddy said, shaking her head and reaching for her drink.

"You're trying to get the dance canceled?" Matt asked.

"Well, it's just that we are supposed to have our soccer fund-raiser on Friday, but now that the dance is the same night, there's no way anyone's gonna show up."

"I think we should just forget the fund-raiser," Emma chimed in. "I mean everyone *I* know is going to the dance. Aren't you guys?"

"Uh, probably not," Matt said.

"Yeah, I doubt it," added Toby.

"Really?" Maddy was intrigued. "It seems like it's all anyone's talking about."

"I think Valentine's Day is kinda dumb," said Matt.

"Me, too!" Maddy responded excitedly.

"You do?" asked Josh. "I thought you just wanted the dance to be on a different night."

"I'm just so sick of hearing about it, is all," said Maddy.

"Well, we're definitely going, aren't we?" Emma turned toward Li and Michele.

"Definitely!" they responded.

"Are you going to start a protest or something?" Matt asked, still interested in Maddy's plans.

"I don't know about a protest, but if you guys have any other ideas . . ." Maddy responded, brightening at the thought that there might still be a chance to save the fund-raiser.

"Come on, girls, I don't want to hear anymore of this anti-Valentine's Day stuff." Emma sounded annoyed. The three girls gathered up their lunch trays and said good-bye. Once they were gone, Josh said, "Yeah, guys, we should try to think of some way to help." He smiled at Maddy again.

"OK, sure. I'll think about it," Toby offered.

"Great!" said Maddy.

Josh gave Maddy another look. *Why does he keep looking at me like that?* she thought. *Oh, no! What if there's something in my teeth?*

Maddy nervously got up from the table. "I just remembered I have to, um, do something before science class. So, uh, why don't we meet in the gym after soccer practice and see if we've come up with anything?"

Josh looked a little disappointed. "Yeah, OK," he said.

"Bye!"

"Bye, Maddy."

Maddy hurried through the lunchroom to dump her tray. Sarah was still at the eighth-grade table and it seemed like she was having a great time. Maddy felt sick to her stomach. It was weird seeing Sarah with other girls. *What if she doesn't even want to be friends anymore?* she thought as she left the cafeteria. *What if . . .*

"Look, it's Mrs. Plimpton!"

Maddy's thoughts were interrupted by the last words she wanted to hear. She looked around expecting to see Monica and her friends, but was greeted by a sneering face she didn't even recognize. Even girls she didn't know were teasing her about Glen Plimpton! Between the weird looks she had been getting for her student council speech and her math quiz grade, Maddy was already feeling bad enough. Now Sarah was eating with a new lunch crowd and Monica had managed to totally revive the Glen Plimpton joke.

The afternoon didn't get much better for Maddy. She was usually pretty good about focusing in school, but not today. She got hit in the head and knocked to the ground during a dodge ball game in gym class. Then she was called on when she wasn't paying attention in science *and* in social studies. She couldn't stop thinking about seeing Sarah in the lunchroom with a completely new group. Sarah had always been so quiet and shy around new people. It really seemed like she was coming out of her shell and making new friends: friends that had nothing to do with Maddy. She even looked like an eighth-grader, sitting at that table.

"Maddy?" Mr. Herron, her social studies teacher, asked again.

"She must be thinking about Glen," Jennifer said. Maddy didn't really know Jennifer that well, but she did know that she took gymnastics with Monica.

I can't believe this is happening again! Maddy's thoughts snapped away from Sarah for a minute. She was furious with her sister. *Maybe I should just transfer to a new school. I'm sure no one at Thomas Gracey Middle School knows about me and Glen Plimpton yet . . .*

"Madeleine Wilkes, I asked you another question," Mr. Herron said for a third time, the irritation in his voice reaching a new high.

"Sorry, Mr. Herron! Can you repeat the question?"

If there was one thing Maddy could focus on, it was soccer. She knew practice would take her mind off of things, at least for a little while. And it felt good to run and kick to get some of her frustration out. She just imagined her sister's face every time the ball came her way.

After practice, Coach Simmons called a team meeting to talk about the fund-raiser.

"I know many of you are concerned that the Valentine's Day Dance is on the same night as our soccer fund-raiser. I just wanted you to know that I'm aware of this and I'm working with Principal Fernandez to figure something out. For now, we are going to cancel Friday's fund-raiser and look at some alternate dates in the near future."

"What? No!" Maddy shouted.

Maddy's dad stepped forward. "Maddy, calm down. Coach Simmons is working really hard on this."

"I just don't think it's fair!" Maddy continued.

"I understand how you feel, Maddy," Coach Simmons added. "But a lot of your teammates are really looking forward to the dance and we can't ignore that, either."

Maddy focused on her sneakers and felt her teammates focusing on her.

"OK, fine," she said, admitting defeat. There was nothing she could do about the Valentine's dance now.

"I will let you all know as soon as Principal Fernandez and I have found another date for the fund-raiser. We'll work something out, don't worry," Coach Simmons finished, looking straight at Maddy.

Everyone started gathering up their soccer gear to leave. Most of the girls on the team were already giggling excitedly about their outfits and making plans for the dance. Before she left, Li offered to help Maddy with her penalty kicks at the next practice. Michele gave Maddy a pat on the back.

"I know you really wanted to do the fund-raiser on Friday, Maddy, but we'll come up with an even better plan for the new one. And at least we won't be stuck in the library!" she said.

Maddy knew Michele was right and she was glad her friends were trying to make her feel better. But she had had her heart set on this event for so long and had loved planning it. She felt like it had been her special project.

Across the gym, Maddy saw Josh standing by the bleachers talking to someone. She expected to see Matt and Toby there as well, but it was just Josh and a girl. Actually, not just a girl — it was Jessica Saunders, eighth-grader, student council president extraordinaire, prettiest and most popular girl in all of Evergreen Middle School, and friend-of-Monica Wilkes talking to Josh!

What is she doing talking to him? Maddy thought. *How do they even know each other? Does she have a crush on Josh?*

Maddy turned away, desperate to escape the gym before Josh saw her.

"Hey, Maddy, wait a sec!"

Too late.

Josh bounded toward her. "Sorry, my friends aren't here."

"Yeah, I noticed that," Maddy replied shortly.

"Well, right after you left the table at lunch today some eighth-grade girl came up and asked Toby to the dance. So Matt decided if Toby was going then he had to go, so he asked your friend Emma."

"Wow, that was fast," Maddy said snidely and then caught herself. "It's alright. Coach Simmons just told us they canceled the fund-raiser, anyway."

"I'm sorry, Maddy. That really stinks."

"It's OK."

Maddy bent down and continued to stuff her soccer cleats into her gym bag.

"So, um, about the dance . . ." Josh mumbled. "I was just wondering, I mean, if . . ."

"What?" Maddy asked, still irritated and now distracted by her dad motioning toward the door. "I have to go, my dad's waiting. See you tomorrow, Josh."

"Bye," Josh sighed.

On the way home from soccer, Maddy's dad kept eyeing her from the driver's seat.

"Are you sure you're OK, Mad?" he asked. "You're pretty quiet over there."

"Yeah, I'm OK." Maddy stared out the side window. She didn't feel OK — she felt terrible, but she just didn't want to talk about it.

As they turned off of Third Street and headed

toward Dogwood, Maddy noticed a small group of girls walking along the sidewalk. She strained to see if she recognized any of them and let out a small noise when she realized she did. It was Sarah. She was with most of the girls from her lunch table that afternoon. They were walking toward Sarah's house. As she passed by, Maddy couldn't decide if she should slump down in the truck and hide or if she should make her presence known and stare out the window. She ended up kind of doing both: slinking down in her seat, but staring right at them. Sarah didn't see her — at least she didn't act like she had. She was laughing and talking in a really animated way, her hands making wide circles in the air. The girls were clustered around her like she was the leader of the group and they seemed desperate to hear what she was saying.

How did this happen? It's like she's forgotten I even exist, Maddy thought. *I can't believe she invited those girls over to her house already.*

That night at dinner Maddy barely spoke. Though Maddy's parents were a little concerned by her silence, Monica was more than happy to make up for any lulls in the conversation. She talked about how she had said something brilliant in her history class that her teacher had just loved. She talked about how she had done a nearly impossible balance beam routine at gymnastics. Mr. and Mrs. Wilkes listened attentively and congratulated Monica on all of her accomplishments. They asked Maddy about her day too, but she just squeaked out a "fine" and continued stacking Tater Tots on top of one another on her plate.

Later that night Maddy clicked open her laptop to erase the fund-raiser announcement from the soccer home page. She checked her e-mail again, hoping Sarah had written. Her in-box was empty except for an invite to the Valentine's Day Dance from one of the student council committees. Maddy covered her face with a pillow. This was turning into the worst *week* of her life.

There was a quick knock at Maddy's door and her dad poked his head in.

"Hi, Dad," Maddy sighed.

"Hey, Mad," he said, entering the room. "I just wanted to make sure you were OK about the whole fund-raiser situation and everything. You were pretty quiet on the ride home and during dinner tonight."

"I guess I'm alright. I just don't get what the big deal is with all this Valentine's Day stuff."

"I know you're frustrated, Maddy, and I know it doesn't make a lot of sense to you right now, but someday you might actually like Valentine's Day, too."

"Ew, no way, Dad," Maddy responded. Her face looked like she just swallowed a lemon.

"I think I was just about your age the first time I realized I liked a girl," Mr. Wilkes continued, smiling slightly. "It was like a switch went off. One day I would have preferred to push this girl down in the mud and then the next day I got tongue-tied around her and didn't know what to do."

Maddy laughed. "Well, I'm too busy to think about boys, Dad. I'd rather play soccer."

"Just try not to be so hard on yourself and on your teammates."

"I'll try not to," Maddy responded.

"And we'll make enough money to go to State, Maddy. Don't you worry."

"Thanks, Dad."

After Maddy's dad left, she checked her chat program to see if Sarah was online. Again she was logged in and chatting away, but not to Maddy. *It's like she has a whole new life that I'm not a part of,* Maddy worried. She stared at the screen for a minute before shutting down her computer. She had no idea what to do about the Sarah situation.

CHAPTER 7

V-Day

When Maddy's alarm went off at 7:15 the next morning, she thought it sounded particularly loud and annoying. In fact, she was convinced it had a higher pitched tone than usual. And then she remembered why: V-Day. The dreaded day had arrived. She pulled her green comforter over her head.

Maybe I can pretend to be sick and stay home, she thought. *No, that won't work. Mom will know I'm faking and Monica will turn it into a chance to humiliate me anyhow.* Her alarm blared again and she scrambled to turn it off.

Maddy slid out of bed trying to exert the least amount of energy possible. She shuffled down the hall to the bathroom and discovered that Monica was still in the shower. *Great. Now I'm going to be late, too.* She could hear Monica singing a song Maddy had just heard on the radio — something about "my baby." She opened the bathroom door as quietly as she could and snuck to the toilet. Her hand hovered over the handle for a second and then she plunged it down and scurried back to the door.

"Ahhhhh!" Monica cried out from the shower. "What hap . . . Maddy!" she screamed.

Maddy giggled and hurried back to her room. She opened her closet and scanned the shelves for something to wear. She selected a pair of black boot-cut jeans and a black turtleneck shirt. Then she found a pair of black socks in her dresser and put on her black Adidas sneakers.

"Perfect," she said as she glanced in the mirror hanging behind her door. "Maybe I can handle V-Day after all."

Before Maddy went back to the bathroom to brush her teeth and try to calm down her crazy curls, she called Pete into her bedroom.

"Peetie! Come 'ere, boy!"

Pete trotted in with a huge smile on his face.

"Well, don't *you* look happy today," Maddy remarked. Then she saw his collar.

"What is this? How could Mom do this to you? Poor Pete."

Pete was wearing a bright pink collar with huge red rhinestone hearts all over it. He actually seemed to be enjoying it quite a bit. Maddy pulled the poster she had drawn out from under her bed and fastened it around Pete's middle with string.

"There you go, Peetie. Now you'll be on my side for sure."

Pete scratched at the sign for a second and then decided he didn't mind it so much, either. He wandered out of Maddy's room and down the stairs.

After Maddy finished flattening her hair with black barrettes, she went down to the kitchen for breakfast. She could hear the music before she even reached the bottom of the stairs: Frank Sinatra's *Greatest Love Songs*. She recognized it instantly. Her mom played it every year on Valentine's Day and on their wedding anniversary. And over the music she could hear her mom's off-key voice emanating from the kitchen. She hesitated to even open the kitchen door, but she knew that there would be fresh-baked muffins inside if she did. As soon as she opened the door, though, she instantly regretted it. Her parents were dancing!

"Mom, Dad, knock it off!" Maddy shouted, but tried not to laugh or smile at the same time.

"Madeleine Sue Wilkes." Mrs. Wilkes stopped and let her hands drop to her sides. "Look at your outfit. Do you really have to be such a stick-in-the-mud, honey?"

"Mom, I'm making a statement."

"Like the one you made on Pete? That poor dog doesn't know what's going on. That thing keeps slipping onto his head and he just ran into the table."

"I'll fix it," Maddy answered, noticing her mom's sweatshirt for the first time. Maddy was pretty sure it was the loudest, most awful Valentine's Day sweatshirt she had ever seen her mom wear. And there had been some pretty bad ones over the years. This one had two fat pink embroidered cupids pointing arrows at each other with a giant red embroidered heart in the middle. Maddy looked to her dad hoping to exchange a knowing glance, but realized even *he* was wearing a red T-shirt for work.

"Dad, you're such a traitor! I can't believe Mom convinced you to wear a red T-shirt to work!" Maddy exclaimed.

"Sorry, Mad, but I've got to stand by the woman I love," Mr. Wilkes replied, dipping Mrs. Wilkes like a salsa dancer.

Mrs. Wilkes giggled and carefully straightened her sweatshirt as she walked over to the counter to pour Maddy a glass of orange juice. Maddy selected a giant blueberry muffin from the tower of fresh baked goods on the counter. She stared at the muffin, trying to figure out what was wrong with it.

"Aren't they adorable? I dyed the batter pink!" Maddy's mom squeaked, handing her the juice.

"Geez, Mom. You're like the V-Day fairy or something," Maddy responded.

"Oh, Maddy, honestly. I don't understand why you're being so silly about this. Why can't you just try to enjoy Valentine's Day? It's not as bad as you think. It's such a fun holiday — maybe you'll get a treat from a secret admirer or something!"

"Um, I don't think so, Mom." Maddy laughed, but then her eyes got very serious. "Besides, I refuse to participate in the holiday that is responsible for ruining my fund-raiser or one that my sister loves so much."

Just then Monica flew through the kitchen door.

"Happy Valentine's Day!" she cried, her hands in the air as if to say 'Ta Da!'.

Maddy tried to take in her outfit. She was wearing red Converse sneakers, white leggings with tiny red hearts all over them, her favorite denim miniskirt, a red fuzzy V-neck sweater with a white tank top underneath, dangly red earrings, and a thin white plastic headband. Maddy felt dizzy just looking at her.

"Ohhhh!" Maddy's mom cooed, running over to Monica's side of the counter to get a better look. "You look absolutely adorable!"

"Isn't this the perf outfit?" Monica responded, twirling in a circle. "Oooo, muffins!"

Maddy slapped her hand to her forehead and tried not to look at Monica's head-spinning ensemble.

Maybe I'm adopted, she thought as she popped a giant pink glob of muffin in her mouth. *That would explain a few things . . .*

"Here's your orange juice, honey," Mrs. Wilkes said, holding out a glass to Monica.

"Oh, thanks, Mom, but I'm leaving early. Emily's sister is picking me up in a sec," she responded as she glanced out the window at the driveway for a third time.

Maddy eyed her suspiciously. "Why are you going to school early?"

"Um, I just have this project to finish with Emily," Monica half mumbled. "Oh! There's Emily and Talia. I gotta go." Monica jumped up from her stool and stuffed half of her muffin in her mouth.

"Dad?" she called with her mouth full. "Don't forget to wait for me after gymnastics. I'm sure I'm going to need a ride home again this year!"

"I won't forget. Am I going to need to rent a U-Haul?" Maddy's dad joked.

"You might want to consider it!" Monica laughed and gave Maddy the biggest, cheesiest smile she possibly could. Last year Monica got so many Valentine's Day gifts — miniature teddy bears holding stuffed hearts, balloon bouquets, flowers, cards, boxes of chocolates, and heart-o-grams — that she couldn't carry them all home.

"Bye-eee!" Monica shouted as she ran out the door, her coat and book bag trailing behind her.

"Bye, honey, happy Valentine's Day!" Mrs. Wilkes called after her.

Maddy glared down at the pink crumbs on her plate. She was annoyed. *She didn't even notice my anti-V-Day outfit*, she thought. *And she probably didn't see Pete, either.*

One second later, Pete strolled into the kitchen and scratched furiously at Maddy's sign until it fell off and then he lay down on top of it. Maddy let out a huge sigh.

She sat at the kitchen table for as long as she could, hoping her parents would forget she was there and she wouldn't have to go to school. Her dad came in and out of the room a few times gathering his lunchbox and work supplies. Finally he said, "Maddy, you're going to be late for school if you sit there much longer."

A few minutes later, Maddy's dad kissed her on the forehead and left for work.

"Get to school," he said. "I'll see you at soccer practice. And Mad, try not to let Valentine's Day get you down. It's just one day. How much harm can it do, huh?"

Then Maddy's mom came back into the kitchen with her coat on. She was carrying a giant basket of Valentine's Day paraphernalia to add to the decorations at the bakery.

"Maddy, what on earth are you still doing here? You're going to be late!"

"I don't know," Maddy mumbled in response.

"Come on, I'll drive you — I've got to get to

the bakery early, anyway, and get busy on our day's orders."

Maddy walked to the sink as if she had cement boots on and rinsed her dishes. She picked up her backpack and her mom practically had to push her out the door. She glanced one more time at Pete hoping he might save her, but he was asleep on the kitchen floor with a piece of string in front of his nose blowing in and out with his breath.

Well, I guess this is it, she thought.

Driving to school, Maddy had an even bigger sense of dread than she had had the day before. Her stomach hurt. Her head felt tight. She knew school was going to be crazy that day. She tried to think of any way to get out of going.

"Don't you need some extra help at the bakery today, Mom? I could help you." Maddy couldn't believe she was volunteering to work at the bakery, but even that was better than school.

"What?" Maddy's mom asked, completely distracted as usual. "Do you need something at the bakery, honey? Did you want to bring some cookies to your friends?"

"No, never mind," Maddy sighed. "You can drop me off right here."

"Now try to have a good day, Maddy. And don't be mean to anyone about Valentine's Day." Mrs. Wilkes tried not to sound worried.

"Don't worry, Mom, I'll keep my mouth shut. Or try to, anyway. Thanks for the ride."

Maddy closed the car door and turned to face the front of Evergreen Middle School. She gave herself a little pep talk as she walked as slowly as possible to the front door.

It's not going to be that bad. Just try to ignore it and avoid Monica if at all possible. The day will be over soon and then you have soccer practice. It will be fine.

The minute she opened the door, though, it was complete chaos. She had only been in the hall for 30 seconds when she got whacked in the face by a giant bouquet of silver Mylar balloons. She had to wade through the groups of girls clustered around lockers squealing about the flower deliveries piling up in the main office or the heart-o-grams they were dying to receive and ones they wished they hadn't sent.

"Should I have sent that one to Joe? Maybe I should try to take it back! What if he doesn't like me? I'm so nervous!"

"But what about the one I sent to Landon? Keena is going to be so mad at me!"

Maddy finally made it to her locker and scrambled to get her morning books into her bag so she could disappear into homeroom. Emma came running up.

"There you are, Maddy. I didn't get a chance to talk to you after soccer practice last night. You'll never guess what happened!"

"What?"

"Your friend Josh's friend Matt asked me to the dance yesterday! Isn't that exciting?"

"That's great." Maddy eked out a reply.

"What's wrong?"

"Nothing, I'm just feeling a little exhausted by this whole V-Day thing."

"Yeah, I kinda noticed from your outfit today. You're so serious about it!"

"Well, I just decided I wanted to make a statement. I don't think it's exactly working, though."

"I really wish you would get over the soccer fund-raiser, Maddy. We'll work it out."

"I know. I'm fine."

"You should just come to the dance with us, it will be fun! Everyone's going to be there," Emma offered.

"Thanks, that's OK." Maddy did appreciate Emma's concern and decided it wasn't fair to be so glum about her news.

"I am happy for you, though," she added.

"Well, I guess I'll see you in class this afternoon," Emma replied.

"OK, bye."

After homeroom Maddy went straight to English class, hoping to have a quiet minute or two. There were only a few other students in the room when she arrived. Just as she was about to sit down at her desk, she noticed something on top of Josh's desk: a heart-o-gram. Curious, Maddy leaned over to get a better look. She gasped in horror as she realized what was written on the front of the heart-o-gram:

Will You Be My Valentine?
Love, Maddy Wilkes ♥

Maddy had no time to think. Her face had already turned as red as a fire truck. She snatched up the heart-o-gram and turned in a circle. The classroom started to fill up. The bell was about to ring. Maddy scanned the room, desperately looking for the trash can or a book of matches or an invisibility machine. She turned again, ready to dash out of the room to flush the heart-o-gram down the toilet, and ran smack into Kyle Lester. As if in slow motion, as her hands moved downward toward her sides, Kyle's hands moved up. Maddy gently placed the heart-o-gram directly into Kyle's waiting hands. Slowly, he looked down and his eyes moved from left to right as he took in the words. Maddy looked down and read the words again, too, still unsure what was actually happening. But there they were, right in front of her: "Will You Be My Valentine? Love, Maddy Wilkes."

Oh my gosh! Maddy screamed inside her head. *It doesn't even say Josh on it. Kyle thinks it's for him!* Kyle raised his head and for a minute looked kind of concerned. Then a huge smile spread across his face. Maddy recognized instantly what was about to happen and there was nothing she could do. Kyle Lester was about to become Kyle *Jester*.

"Well, well, well," Kyle boomed. He looked around to make sure people were paying attention. "What do we have here?"

Just then, three students filed into the room as if on cue from the director: Sarah Warren, Josh Martin, and Glen Plimpton.

"Will you be my valentine? Love, Maddy Wilkes," Kyle recited at the top of his lungs. "Gosh, Maddy, I don't know what to say!" he continued, his own face getting a little bit red. "But what about Glen, Maddy?"

Maddy could hear snickering around her. She stood frozen to her spot. It was like she was watching someone else be her.

Glen was thrilled to hear his name enter the conversation.

"Uh, yeah, Maddy, what about me?" he asked, stepping to Kyle's side. "I thought *I* was your valentine?"

Now everyone in the class was laughing, except for Sarah and Josh, who stood next to each other near the door of the room.

"No, I . . . it was . . ." Maddy tried to speak. She couldn't even make her mouth form a word. She was still trying to figure out how this could be happening.

The bell rang and everyone moved toward their seats. Both Kyle and Glen continued to make kissing noises at Maddy. Several girls asked if they should call her Mrs. Plimpton or Mrs. Lester now.

Sarah looked like she was either going to hit Maddy or burst into tears. Maddy knew Sarah had seen what just happened, and she knew Sarah was mad. *Does she really think I like Kyle?* Maddy wondered. *Maybe she thinks I am trying to get back at her for the whole student council thing.*

Maddy watched Sarah move like a robot toward her desk. She was wearing a soft pink long-sleeved shirt and a black skirt. Her outfit was paired with pink-and-black plaid knee-high socks and black flats. She had pink heart-shaped earrings in her ears and her dark brown hair hung perfectly straight and shiny down her back. Sarah had a hint of light pink gloss on her lips.

She looks so pretty, Maddy thought, *and so sophisticated.* Maddy wanted desperately to grab Sarah's arm and run to the bathroom to explain everything. She would have given her right leg, no, that was her kicking leg, her *left* leg, to be hanging out with Sarah as if nothing had ever happened. All she wanted right now was to be at home, in her bedroom, with Sarah sitting on her bed talking about a new fabric she found or the skirt pattern she was working on. But instead, she was in her English class with a whole room of people laughing at her and there was no way Sarah was going anywhere with her.

Josh darted by Maddy and slid into his seat without saying a word. He quickly stuffed a piece of drawing paper in his backpack and took out his English book.

Most of the class was still laughing and talking as Mr. Anderson walked to the front of the room.

"OK, everyone. Settle down."

Thank you, Mr. A. At least someone can put a stop to this, Maddy thought as she pushed herself further down into her seat, her heart pounding a million times a minute. *For the second year in a row, I am completely humiliated on Valentine's Day. I'm cursed. I should have known!*

"Let's open to chapter seven and read a little Shakespeare today, shall we?" Mr. Anderson said. "In honor of the occasion, I thought we might recite a few love sonnets." He continued with a smile on his face. "What do you say, Maddy, want to start us off?"

Maddy's face flamed to life again. "Um, do I have to?" she mumbled.

"Come on, Maddy, show a little love!" Mr. Anderson joked and everyone laughed.

Why can't I just close my eyes and magically be at soccer practice right now? Maddy thought as she reluctantly opened her anthology.

"Um, where should I start?" Maddy asked.

"Why don't you just start with number one and we'll see how far you get?" Mr. Anderson suggested, still smiling.

Maddy groaned and closed her eyes for a minute, hoping somehow she'd open them and be on the soccer field. But, she opened them to her entire English class staring straight at her and waiting for her to start the sonnets.

CHAPTER 8

The Realization

That afternoon, Maddy had endured much of the same teasing as she had all week. Word of the heart-o-gram spread as fast as any gossip around Evergreen did. Now Maddy's classmates were calling her both "Mrs. Lester" and "Mrs. Plimpton" and congratulating her on having two boyfriends. She decided to eat lunch in the library to avoid any cafeteria scenes with Kyle or Glen, but of course Glen met with his chess club in the library on Wednesdays. He started to make smoochy faces and called to Maddy the minute he saw her come in. Luckily Mrs. Ward, the librarian, was quick to warn Glen about noise, so Maddy retreated to the computer lab and ate her sandwich there.

She didn't feel like seeing Sarah at the eighth-grade table again, either. She was probably telling all her new friends what a traitor and a backstabber Maddy was. Maddy was sure Sarah recounted the entire story about what happened in Mr. Anderson's class that morning. She imagined the other girls crowding around Sarah, giving her hugs of encouragement and telling her to forget all about horrible Maddy Wilkes.

Marc Tyson even tried to serenade Kyle and Maddy in social studies, but luckily Mr. Herron had put a stop to it. Though Maddy had successfully managed to avoid Monica all day (that was probably the only good thing that had happened), Monica's friends wasted no time joining in the teasing. They embarrassed Maddy any chance they got — including bursting into the gym during her gym class and calling to her about her crushes in front of the entire class. Of course, Maddy was hanging from the middle of the rope climb at that moment.

By the end of the day, for the first time ever, Maddy didn't even *want* to be at soccer practice. After everything that had happened the last few days, she felt totally miserable. When Maddy had walked into Evergreen that morning, she was sure there was no way things could have gotten worse, but they definitely had. Not only had she and Sarah been fighting all week, but now Sarah thought Maddy was trying to steal her crush! Nothing could have been further from the truth. Maddy still couldn't figure out who gave that heart-o-gram to Josh with her name on it. She felt totally alone and all she could think about was how she needed her best friend Sarah to talk to — but Sarah was the one person who might never talk to Maddy again.

After soccer practice, Maddy's dad and Coach Simmons needed to finalize the team's upcoming schedule, so Maddy milled around the gym hoping Josh might come over to talk but he didn't. His team was still practicing on the other field, so Maddy decided to walk over to talk to him. She needed to see a familiar face and someone who wouldn't tease her like everyone else. She also wanted to say something about the whole episode with Kyle in English class, but she had no idea how to begin. Josh was kicking the ball around with Matt at the far end of the gym.

"Hi, Josh! Hi, Matt!" Maddy called from the side of the field as she approached them.

"Hi, Maddy," Matt replied.

"Hey, Maddy," said Josh, more to himself than to her.

"How's your practice going?" Maddy asked, struggling to think of something more interesting to ask.

"Um, fine, we're just still in the middle of doing stuff so . . ." Josh trailed off.

"Oh well, I just thought I'd come over and see how it was going." Maddy had no idea what else to say.

"Well, I can't really talk right now," Josh said without looking over.

"Oh, alright, I guess I'll just see ya later then, I guess." Embarrassed, Maddy turned back toward the other field. *That was weird. Is Josh mad at me?* she wondered. *Why would he be mad? If anyone has a right to be mad, it's me! Why didn't he try to stick up for me in English today?*

Maddy ran back to where her dad and Coach Simmons were talking. Her face was bright red again. She hoped it was at least turning a different shade of red each time she had been embarrassed today — to keep things interesting at least.

"Ready, Mad? I guess we can go wait for your sister in the truck," said Mr. Wilkes.

"Yes, good idea," Maddy responded quickly. She couldn't wait to get out of there.

"So, how did it go today? It wasn't too bad, right?" Maddy's dad asked once they were situated in the parking lot.

"You don't even want to know, Dad, believe me," responded Maddy. At this point, she didn't know whether to laugh or cry.

"Well, it couldn't have been as bad as it was for George at work," Mr. Wilkes chuckled. "He forgot about Valentine's Day altogether and had to scramble around at lunchtime trying to figure out what he could get for his wife on such short notice.

It was pretty funny. The poor guy even tried to buy this . . ."

Maddy tuned out her dad's voice the minute she spotted Josh walking across the parking lot with Jessica Saunders. They walked slowly and in step with each other and looked deep in conversation. For a second, Maddy even thought they were holding hands, but they weren't. She couldn't believe they were hanging out again. Maddy had thought maybe that time in the gym was just a random thing — like Jessica was lost and needed directions and Josh was the only person in a ten-mile radius that she could ask for help.

What could they possibly be talking about? Maddy wondered. *Why is she even giving him the time of day? He's just a seventh-grader!* Maddy's stomach started to hurt. *Does Josh like her? Does Jessica like* him? *What are they talking about!?* Maddy felt a growing nervousness in her chest that she hadn't ever felt before. Her heart was beating fast. *What's wrong with me? Why am I freaking out like this? What do I care if Josh and*

Jessica Saunders are friends . . . or more. I mean, Josh and I are friends . . . . We're good friends, I think. He's really funny and such a great artist — I loved that drawing of the meteor and the school he did. And he's the best soccer player I know (well, that I know personally, he's not better than Pelé or Beckham, but still). We had so much fun at soccer camp last summer. And he's always been super nice in class. I love how he is always flipping his hair out of his eyes and . . . Maddy's heart skipped a little bit. *Oh, my gosh. I do like Josh Martin. I do have a crush on him! But I don't even know how to have a crush! What if I can't be normal around him now? What if it ruins our friendship? WHAT IF HE DOESN'T LIKE ME BACK?* She felt panicked. She gripped the edge of the seat and looked around her dad's truck as if there might be something there to help her, some sort of magic wand that would stop her heart from beating out of her chest.

"You alright, Mad?" Mr. Wilkes gave Maddy a weird look.

"Uh-huh," Maddy said breathlessly.

Now the idea of Josh and Jessica Saunders liking each other was too much for Maddy to handle. She wanted to run across the parking lot and break up their conversation. She wanted to put Jessica in a plastic bubble for the next five months until she graduated to Hamilton High School. She wanted to erase her from Josh's memory completely. Then something else occurred to Maddy for the tenth time that day: *I need Sarah. She would know exactly how to deal with this.*

Mr. Wilkes let out a half-groan, half-laugh, snapping Maddy out of the drama swirling around in her mind. He was shaking his head and pointing toward the door of the gym. Maddy turned and she saw a giant mass of stuff with two tiny legs covered in white leggings with red hearts on them heading toward the truck. It was Monica with her armload of V-Day gifts. Maddy couldn't even see her head, just the piles and piles of stuffed animals, balloons, gift boxes, and flowers.

"Ugh," Maddy grunted. "I can't believe her."

Just then it hit her: Monica. *She* was the one who left the heart-o-gram on Josh's desk! How did she not see it before? That thick bubbly handwriting! The giant pink heart after her name! And Monica had acted so strangely this morning — going to school early and everything.

She must have heard me in the kitchen the other day telling Mom about my fight with Sarah and how Sarah accused me of liking Josh! Maddy realized. *I can't believe she did this to me* again!

Monica opened the door to the truck and started to dump her loot onto the seat.

"Hi-eee!" she screeched. "Isn't this just crazy?"

Maddy reached out toward the biggest, pinkest balloon in one of the balloon bouquets and clapped her hands together as hard as she could. *POP.*

"Hey! What was that for?" Monica looked totally wounded and surprised.

"*That* was for being the worst sister in the history of the entire world," Maddy responded flatly.

Monica finished stuffing the rest of the balloons into the cab of the truck. "What are you talking about, Maddy?" she asked, with the most innocent expression on her face.

"Don't play dumb with me, Monica. I know it was you!" Maddy screamed.

"OK, OK," Mr. Wilkes interjected. "I have no idea what's going on here, but I do know that there is way too little space in this truck to be screaming at each other. You both need to keep quiet until we get home. I don't care if you have to hold your breath — I don't want to hear one word!" Mr. Wilkes looked sternly at both girls and steered the truck out of the parking lot.

Maddy sat stick-straight and kept her eyes on the windshield in front of her. Out of the corner of her eye, though, she could see Monica sifting through all her V-Day junk. Monica giggled quietly at a couple of cards and smelled each different flower individually a million times. Maddy was absolutely fuming. She couldn't wait to get home so she could scream her lungs out at Monica.

Mr. Wilkes pulled into the driveway and gathered up the soccer gear to take to the garage. Monica took what Maddy thought was about twenty years to get herself and all of her things out of the truck. Maddy kicked a couple of stuffed animals out of her way as she slid out of the truck and stormed into the house.

"Mommmm!" she bellowed from the front hall.

Mrs. Wilkes came tearing out of the kitchen. She had so much flour in her hair it looked white — like she'd aged thirty years that afternoon or was doing a play about George Washington.

"What, Maddy, what? What happened?" she asked as she tried to retie her apron behind her.

"You are not going to believe what happened today. You know how Monica was acting all weird this morning and left early for school?"

"Um, yeah, I guess so," Mrs. Wilkes responded, not sure that she did remember.

"Well, she didn't have a project to finish. She went and planted a valentine on Josh Martin's desk so he would think it was from me!" Maddy said all in one breath.

"Oh, honey, that's sweet," Mrs. Wilkes started to say as she tried to clear flour dust from the air around her. It was beginning to form a cloud.

"MOM!" Maddy screamed. "No, it isn't. It's not sweet at all! She totally did it to be mean and embarrass me in front of my whole class! And it worked!"

There was a knock at the door. Mrs. Wilkes looked to Maddy, expecting her to open it. Maddy crossed her arms and stood right where she was. She knew exactly who was knocking. Exasperated, Mrs. Wilkes crossed the room, her flour cloud hovering around her, and opened the front door.

"Mom, help! I'm about to drop all this stuff," said Monica.

"Oh, goodness! Here, give me the stuffed monkey and the 'I Love You' balloons. OK, got it? Careful . . ." Mrs. Wilkes responded, backing into the room and letting Monica pass by.

"Let's put all this stuff in the dining room for now. Monica, Maddy would like to talk to you about what happened today."

Maddy stormed into the dining room after her mom and Monica.

"Actually, I would be fine never speaking to Monica again. I can't stand that she's my sister! She's been tormenting me at school for years and this just tops it off. Mom, you have to do something!"

Monica stood next to her pile of V-Day treats and stared at Maddy. Then she turned toward Mrs. Wilkes and softened her eyes. "Mom, I was only trying to help. I heard Maddy say she liked Josh Martin and I knew she would never do anything about it, so I just wanted to help. That's all . . ."

"See, Maddy, Monica wanted to . . ."

"Mom, don't tell me you believe her!" Maddy shrieked, tears now streaming down her face. "She was trying to humiliate me, AGAIN, in front of my friends and my classmates. I got teased all day and now Sarah totally hates me!" Maddy flopped down in one of the dining room chairs.

"Wait, why does Sarah hate you?" Monica asked. "I thought she liked Kyle Jester, I mean Lester, not Josh."

"She *does* like Kyle. I bumped into Kyle when I was trying to get rid of the heart-o-gram and he thought it was for him! You didn't put Josh's name on it, only mine," Maddy explained through her tears and sobs.

Mrs. Wilkes walked over and put a floury hand on Maddy's shoulder. "I'm sorry, sweetheart — I didn't realize how upset you were about this. And I know you and Sarah have been having a hard time." She turned toward Monica. "Monica, you owe Maddy a huge apology and I think we need to discuss some sort of punishment here. Your sister is very upset."

"Mom, no! She's just being a baby. I was *trying* to help her, but she's hopeless!" Monica tried to defend herself.

"That's enough," Mrs. Wilkes said firmly. "Go to your room, Monica. We'll talk about this after dinner.

Maddy, you go get cleaned up, too. Dinner will be ready soon."

Monica lingered in the dining room trying to pick up all of her V-Day stuff to bring up to her room. Maddy took the stairs two at a time and ran to her bedroom. She slammed the door and locked it. She didn't want to talk to anyone — except for Sarah. She wiped the tears from her face and blew her nose. Then she picked up the phone and dialed Sarah's cell phone number. It rang five times and went to voice mail. Maddy flipped open her laptop and logged in to her chat program, hoping to catch Sarah online so she could explain everything. She wasn't logged in. In one last effort, Maddy dialed Sarah's home line. Jack answered.

"Hullo?"

"Hi, Jack, it's Maddy. Is Sarah home? I really need to talk to her."

"Um . . ."

Maddy could hear talking in the background. It was Sarah telling Jack what to say.

"Um, she's not here now. Can I take a medicine?"

"A what?"

More mumbling in the background.

"A message. I meant message."

Maddy sighed. "Just tell her that Maddy called and it's really important for her to call me back."

"OK bye," Jack said quickly and hung up.

Maddy and Sarah usually did homework together on Wednesday nights. They would talk as soon as Maddy got home from soccer practice and make a plan to meet at one of their houses after dinner. Maddy knew that wouldn't be happening tonight. And maybe not any other night, either.

Dinner at the Wilkes's that night was a little tense. Mrs. Wilkes had made individual heart-shaped pizzas that she was very excited about (also made from pink dough, of course). She talked about how busy her day at the bakery was and how much the couple who got married loved their cake. Mr. Wilkes told his story about George forgetting Valentine's Day and everyone laughed. But other than that, Monica and Maddy both sat silently and picked at their heart pizzas. Mrs. Wilkes had brought home extra cupcakes from the bakery for dessert. Maddy asked if she could take hers up to her room instead of eating it at the table. Though her parents usually wanted the family to finish dinner together, they let her this time. And they decided it would be a good time to discuss Monica's punishment.

Maddy could hear her parents talking over the situation with Monica as she walked up to her room. She thought she would be excited that Monica was getting in trouble, or at least feel a little bit satisfied by it, but she didn't. She didn't even want to sit on the stairs and try to listen, like she usually did. All she could think about was Sarah and how she wanted desperately to talk to her — about their fight and about Josh!

Maddy went to her desk and sat in front of her computer. She took a bite of her cupcake and set it gently to the side. She logged in to the chat program again and there was still no Sarah. She minimized her soccer ball icon at the bottom of the screen and opened her journal. She hadn't written much about the week yet and wanted to get out some of her feelings about the whole Josh situation and being teased all day. Maddy typed for a while — letting out all her anger and frustration.

Monica just makes me so mad. She is constantly trying to embarrass me and get the better of me . . .

Maddy's chat icon popped up from the bottom of the screen.

kyle247: maddy?

mad4soccer: yeah?

kyle247: hey it's kyle

mad4soccer: hi kyle

kyle247: i hope u rn't mad that i teased u 2day

kyle247: i feel bad . . .

mad4soccer: it's OK . . .

Maddy didn't know what to say. She would have never expected Kyle to IM her *and* apologize!

kyle247: i guess i was embarrassed or something
kyle247: but it was nice of u . . .

Awkward screen silence.
What should I do? Maddy thought.

kyle247: i was wondering tho if u wud mind if i asked sarah 2 the v day dance . . .

Maddy couldn't believe it — Kyle liked Sarah, too! She was going to be so excited.

mad4soccer: that's gr8t! u def shud!
kyle247: yur not mad?
mad4soccer: why wud i b?
kyle247: the heart-o-gram . . .
mad4soccer: oh yeah that

mad4soccer: it actually wasn't meant 4 u. it was 4 josh

"Ah! Why did I say that?" Maddy shouted to her computer screen.

kyle247: really? well well . . .

mad4soccer: it wasn't really 4 him either

kyle247: huh?

mad4soccer: never mind. it's a long story . . .

kyle247: so do u think sarah will say yes?

mad4soccer: i know she will!

kyle247: sweet.

kyle247: thx maddy

mad4soccer: no prob. gld i cud help!

kyle247: c u 2mrow

mad4soccer: k bye

Maddy minimized her icon again and sat back in her chair. She was so relieved! The Kyle situation had worked itself out so much better than she thought possible. And Sarah was going to be so excited! Maddy forgot all about her anti-V-Day feelings for a minute. She opened up her journal again and starting reviewing what she had typed. She felt the negativity of her words creeping back over her. She read her entry a few times and realized she didn't like what she was reading. *That doesn't even sound like me!* Maddy thought. *I've never been this negative or angry about anything before. I can't believe I let Valentine's Day and a silly school dance affect me like this.* Then Maddy thought about Monica and their rivalry. She started to understand that the more upset she got about Glen and the teasing, the more Monica enjoyed it and the more *Monica* was in the spotlight instead of Maddy. *She just wants attention*, Maddy suddenly realized. *If I stop giving her so much attention, then maybe she'll get bored and leave me alone!* Maddy felt like she was having this realization for the first time ever. She had never really thought about the fact that she played a role in the teasing, too. *She* let it get worse by showing so much anger and frustration.

Maddy thought about her black outfit that day and her speech to the student council. *Maybe I did go a little overboard on the whole anti-V-Day thing . . . Mom was right — I do tend to get worked up over things.* Maddy thought about Li and Emma and Michele. They cared about the soccer team and the state tournament just as much as she did. But they also cared about the dance. She knew they would find a way to raise the money they needed to go to State.

Then Maddy pictured her parents dancing in the kitchen that morning and thought about how happy they were. She thought about how excited her mom got about holidays and how much she enjoyed designing cakes and desserts and having the bakery.

I need to stop being so negative! Maddy decided. *Valentine's Day is not that big of a deal and if I don't let Monica get to me, then it shouldn't be that bad.* She felt like a huge weight had been lifted from her. She breathed in a deep breath and closed her journal. It was getting late. She would write a new, better entry tomorrow.

Maddy opened her chat list again to sign out and noticed that Josh was logged in. Just then she heard Monica stomping up the stairs and toward her bedroom door. She turned in her chair expecting to hear a knock. Instead, Monica burst through the door. Her face was tear-streaked and puffy.

"Thanks a lot, Maddy!" she cried.

"What did *I* do?" Maddy asked, totally caught off guard.

"Mom and Dad won't let me go to the Valentine's Dance now. *That's* my punishment!" Monica turned and stomped out of the room, slamming the door behind her.

Dazed, Maddy turned back to her computer. Josh's name sat highlighted on her chat list. *What should I do? Should I send him a message? Should I stay on and see if he sends me one? But he seemed so weird this afternoon . . . And then that whole Jessica thing.* Maddy had no idea what to do. She quickly moved her cursor to the "sign out" button and closed the screen. *I'm not ready to deal with "crush Josh" yet — I can still only handle "friend Josh" — at least until I get some advice from Sarah!*

Maddy took a deep breath and decided to confront Monica. Her door was closed and Maddy could hear her crying inside. She thought about bursting in as Monica had, but decided to knock.

"Come in," Monica's voice sounded small and crackled a little bit.

Maddy slowly pushed open the door, still unsure if she actually even wanted to talk to her now. Monica sat up on her bed.

"What?" she said, wiping at her red eyes.

"I came to tell you that I'm sorry about the dance, but you know, *you're* the one who should be apologizing to *me*! Have you even thought about why you're in trouble? Have you stopped thinking about yourself for even a second?" Maddy felt taller than she normally did around Monica.

Monica picked awkwardly at her comforter.

"You need to stop being such a jerk to me all the time!" Maddy said sternly.

Monica kept her eyes on her comforter and didn't say a word. Maddy lingered for a minute for emphasis and then closed the door and went to brush her teeth. She looked in the bathroom mirror and smiled. Just then she felt even older than Monica.

Maddy climbed into bed that night feeling better than she had all week. *Now I just have to get to Sarah first thing tomorrow and explain everything. I need my BFF back!* she thought as she turned out the light.

CHAPTER 9

The News

The next morning Maddy woke up before her alarm. She had slept better than she had in days. She had even had a dream that she and Sarah were playing soccer together. Sarah was wearing her pointy black boots and tons of eye make-up and Maddy was wearing her bathing suit and a hat with a giant cupcake on it, which was really weird, but Maddy was just happy to have had a dream about the two of them hanging out!

She went down the hall to the bathroom and turned on the shower. This was the first time in months she'd gotten into the bathroom before Monica and could shower before the hot water ran out. *Things are looking up!* she thought.

Maddy chose a light yellow wool sweater and her favorite jeans to wear. She even wore her newest pair of Adidases, the ones that weren't too scuffed up or dirty yet, and a pair of green-and-yellow striped socks. She put a tiny pair of emerald earrings (her birthstone) in her ears, then tied her curls back in a low ponytail and went down to the kitchen. Her parents were both seated at the kitchen table, swapping sections of the newspaper and drinking coffee.

"Good. I'm glad you're both here," Maddy said. "I have something I'd like to speak to you about."

"Good morning, Ms. Serious Pants," Mrs. Wilkes responded, chuckling.

"Morning, Mad. Feeling better?" asked Mr. Wilkes.

Maddy stood a little straighter than usual. "I'm trying very hard to have a more positive attitude."

"Well, that's nice!" Mrs. Wilkes gave Maddy a huge smile.

"And I'm sorry I was so anti-Valentine's Day this year. I know it's an important holiday to you guys and I was really negative about it."

"That's OK, Maddy. We know you were upset about the soccer fund-raiser," Mr. Wilkes replied. "And now we also know you were upset about

Monica's behavior at school. We've spoken to her about it." Mr. Wilkes gave Maddy an extra-serious look to be sure she knew they weren't taking Monica's behavior lightly.

"Yeah . . . about that," Maddy started. "I mean, don't get me wrong, I was really mad at Monica. And I'm still not totally over it, but I know how much she wants to go to that dance. And I would feel pretty bad if she didn't get to go, so maybe there's something else she can have as a punishment instead?"

Maddy's parents exchanged quick glances.

"Well, I don't know. We want her to realize her actions have serious consequences . . ." started Mrs. Wilkes.

"I have a few punishment ideas," Maddy chimed in. "She could do my soccer laundry, or bring me lunch in the cafeteria for a week, or wash my feet after every soccer game, or do my math homework for a month, or set the table *and* clear the dinner dishes for a year . . ."

"OK . . . so clearly you've thought about this," Mr. Wilkes laughed. "I guess we can discuss an alternative punishment with Monica if that's the way you feel."

"I know it's weird, but I want Monica to go to the dance." Maddy shrugged. "I do think those are some good ideas, though, of other punishments . . ."

"I think we can come up with something suitable, don't you worry, Maddy." Mr. Wilkes winked.

Mrs. Wilkes got up to fill her coffee cup. "What would you like for breakfast, Maddy? I can make a couple of eggs, or there's toast and fruit."

"Can I just grab a granola bar?" Maddy asked. "I really need to find Sarah before school starts and we haven't been walking together in the mornings."

"Sure, honey, that's fine. I hope everything's OK."

"Thanks, Mom. I think it will be soon," Maddy said as she walked into the hall to get her coat. Monica was coming down the stairs.

"Can I talk to you for a minute, Maddy?" Monica asked.

"Yeah," Maddy responded, a little apprehensively.

"I just wanted to say I'm sorry. I didn't mean to make your day so miserable yesterday. I just thought it would be funny, but I was wrong."

"I forgive you."

"You do?" Monica was surprised.

"You're my only sister, aren't you? What else am I going to do?" Maddy said, half smiling.

"Thanks, Maddy." Monica smiled back.

"Just no more of this Mrs. Plimpton or Mrs. Lester business, OK?"

"OK."

Monica opened the kitchen door and Maddy called over her head, "Don't forget about my suggestions for Monica!"

"What suggestions?" Monica asked as the door closed behind her.

Maddy bundled her green scarf close to her face and hurried along the sidewalk to school. It had started snowing just a little bit. She kept looking behind her to see if Sarah was also walking. She couldn't believe they hadn't walked to or from school together since Monday's fight. That was the most school days they'd ever been apart except for the time in fifth grade when Maddy had had the stomach flu. She hated feeling so distant from Sarah.

As Maddy got closer to Evergreen she also started feeling more and more nervous about seeing Josh. *What if he knows I have a crush on him now? What if he can just sense it?* she thought.

When she got to the building, she headed straight for Sarah's locker, but she wasn't there. Maddy lingered, hoping Sarah would arrive any minute, but she started getting worried that she would be late for homeroom. Maddy took the long way to her own locker, scanning the halls for Sarah, but there was no sign of her. She fidgeted through homeroom, her stomach doing somersaults as she thought about seeing Josh in English class.

By the time Maddy arrived at the door to her English room, she was a wreck. Her heart was pounding so hard she was sure people could see it through her sweater. Her hands were sweaty and she felt dizzy. She even considered going to the school nurse instead of class, but how could she explain what her problem was? When she opened the door just before the final bell, though, the two people she was both dying to see and dreaded seeing, weren't there. She hovered near the door thinking maybe she'd entered the wrong room. But no, Kyle was there, Glen was there, Michele was there. Everyone was there, except Sarah and Josh. She had been so worried about seeing both of them, but now that they weren't in class, Maddy was really disappointed. *Are they* both *trying to avoid me this much?* she worried.

"Don't be shy, Maddy," Mr. Anderson called from the front of the room, gesturing toward her empty desk. "You're still welcome here."

Maddy grimaced at her teacher. *Even Mr. A. seems to enjoy teasing me this week.*

"Unless you'd rather sit by Kyle," Stewart Graham added and everyone laughed.

Maddy reminded herself to straighten up. She made her face relax and took off her backpack. "That's alright, my desk is just fine," she said as she marched confidently to her spot.

"Great, then let's get started," Mr. Anderson said. "No more love poems today, we're on to memoirs. Please open to chapter nine."

That wasn't so bad, Maddy thought. *I can handle this!*

Maddy managed to make it through the rest of the morning with a pretty positive attitude. She was definitely still teased a bunch, but she took it in stride and tried to laugh it off as much as she could. Right after English class, Glen tried making kissy noises at her and she even joked back, leaning her face forward to pretend she *wanted* Glen to kiss her. He practically ran down the hall to hide his embarrassment. She even passed Monica and her friends in the hall before math and the girls kept quiet. Marisol actually said hello to

Maddy and Monica gave Maddy a grateful smile. Their parents must have told Monica about their discussion with Maddy that morning.

After math class, Maddy hurried to the lunchroom. She was sure she could at least find Sarah at her new eighth-grade lunch table. But Sarah's table was practically empty when Maddy arrived — just two of the girls who normally sat there were eating.

"Um, hey," Maddy said quietly. She couldn't believe how intimidated she felt approaching them. "Have you guys seen Sarah Warren?"

The girls stared at Maddy for a second before answering. "Yeah, she's at a decorating committee meeting."

"Oh, OK, thanks," Maddy replied. She had forgotten that all the student council committees were having their last-minute meetings about the dance today.

"Sure, no problem," said one of the girls, who Maddy was sure was an eighth-grader.

She turned on her heel and surveyed the rest of the room. She contemplated going to the computer lab to eat again, but then she spotted Michele, Emma, and Li eating with Toby and Matt across the room. *That's weird,* she thought. *Josh's friends are eating with my friends, but we're not even around.*

Maddy slowly crossed the cafeteria to their table.

"Hey, Maddy!" Emma shouted before she was even halfway there.

"Hey, guys, mind if I join you?" she asked when she arrived.

"Of course not," Emma responded. She was totally beaming. "You know Matt and Toby."

"Yeah, hi."

"Hey, Maddy," they responded together.

"Um, have you guys seen Josh today?" she asked them, her face heating up.

Luckily, Matt was distracted by the giant sub sandwich on his plate. "Yeah, I saw him just before math. He said something about how he was late for school this morning and then had something to take care of at lunch . . . I'm not sure what he was talking about."

"Oh, OK, I was just wondering . . ." Maddy trailed off. *He's totally avoiding me! I can't believe it. Is he not going to come to English class for the rest of the year? He has* to!

"Maddy?" Michele asked.

Maddy looked up and realized the whole table was watching her.

"Huh?" she responded.

"Did you hear me?" Michele asked again, her face twisted into a concerned look.

"No, sorry. What?" Maddy tried to pull herself out of her thoughts.

"I just said you look nice today. Your sweater is really springy."

"Oh, thanks."

Li was staring at Maddy, too. "Yeah, that's quite a change from what you were wearing yesterday."

"I know. I just thought it might be nice. I was a little too intense yesterday, I think. . . . Well, this whole week probably."

"That's for sure!" exclaimed Emma. "Glad to see you're back to your old self!"

Maddy couldn't believe it had been that noticeable! She smiled back at her friends, but they were no longer looking at her. They all had slightly shocked looks on their faces and were staring just over Maddy's left shoulder.

"What's wrong, you guys?" Maddy asked. Then she felt a tap on her shoulder. It was Monica. She was holding a giant chocolate chip cookie. Monica's friend Emily was standing behind her, swaying awkwardly from side to side and nervously glancing at the other tables near Maddy's as if someone might jump out and attack her.

"Hey, Maddy," Monica said, almost seeming shy.

"Hi. What are you doing?"

"I brought you this," Monica said, extending the cookie. "I just wanted to say thanks for talking to Mom and Dad this morning. You didn't have to do that."

"I know."

"Well, thanks. I really appreciate it. And I'm sorry about . . . you know."

Maddy took the cookie and watched as Monica walked back to her "most-popular-eighth-grade-girls" table across the room. Now she shared the same shocked expression her friends had.

"Who was *that*?" Toby asked, barely able to close his mouth.

"*That* was Maddy's sister!" Michele said in disbelief. "I've never even seen you guys *talk* at school!"

"Yeah," Li joined in. "That was crazy."

Maddy totally agreed. It was crazy. But she didn't want to make too big of a deal of it. "Yeah, well, we just had some things to work out." She broke off a piece of the cookie. "Want some?" she asked, holding it out to her friends. Emma, Li, and Michele each broke off a tiny bite, then Matt and Toby grabbed the rest and shoved it into their mouths. Maddy laughed and picked up her fork. Her macaroni and cheese was getting cold.

Despite worrying about the situation with Sarah and Josh, Maddy sailed through her afternoon. She was really enjoying her more stress-free school day and couldn't believe it had taken her so long to figure out that she was being so negative about everything. Monica's lunchroom apology had certainly helped her mood as well.

She still hadn't seen either Sarah or Josh, though, and was worried about when she'd get a chance to. She was dying to hear Sarah's reaction to being asked to the dance by Kyle. She was sure Sarah already had the perfect outfit planned. And she really wanted to talk to Josh about a new idea she'd had: combining the girls' and boys' soccer fund-raisers into one big event and splitting the proceeds. That would give her a chance to work closely on a project with Josh! Deep in thought about asking Josh over to her house to work on the soccer project, Maddy turned the corner to enter the gym after school and collided with Kyle Lester and Glen Plimpton. Maddy's backpack fell to the ground, Kyle's notebook sprung open and papers went everywhere, and Glen's glasses flew across the floor.

"Geez, Maddy, we've got to stop meeting like this," Kyle joked.

Glen walked away to retrieve his glasses and let out a flood of laughter that sounded like a chicken being strangled. "That's a good one, Kyle. I should write that down."

"Glen was just telling me about some of his new stand-up comedy material," Kyle explained, rolling his eyes a bit.

"Oh, how interesting." Maddy smiled. She was surprised by how relaxed she felt! "So how did it go asking Sarah to the dance?"

"Well, it hasn't actually gone yet! I was just going to ask you if you'd seen her today. I was planning to ask her right after English this morning, but then she wasn't there. I've looked everywhere for her!"

Maddy shook her head. "Yeah, you're not the only one. I haven't seen her, either."

"I'm worried someone else might ask her and I *really* want to go . . . I mean it would be cool and everything if it worked out." Kyle shifted nervously from one foot to the other and jammed his hands into his pockets.

"Well, you should just call her!" Maddy suggested. "I can give you her cell number if you don't have it."

"Really? That would be awesome." Kyle beamed.

Maddy took a pen and a scrap of notebook paper out of her backpack and wrote Sarah's number down for Kyle. She handed him the paper and smiled. "Call her now!"

"OK, I'm going to do it right now."

Kyle finished gathering all his notebook paper and bounded out of the gym. "Glen, buddy, I'll see you later!"

"Oh, yeah, sure, OK, Kyle. Talk to you later or something. We can catch up about my jokes tomorrow or whatever," Glen yelled after him.

"Well, I gotta go, too, Glen. I've got soccer practice," said Maddy, relieved she also had an excuse.

"Alright, Maddy, bye then. OK, bye," Glen stammered, also seeming relieved not to be alone with her after the near-kiss incident that morning.

Maddy was on fire during soccer practice. She couldn't wait for Saturday's game. If she could keep this momentum up, she would be the star of the team in no time and then Josh would notice her for sure!

"Wow, Maddy, looking good!" Coach Simmons called from the sidelines.

"Thanks, coach!" Maddy smiled and ran faster.

The team worked on kicking and passing drills and then ran a few laps to finish up the practice. Most of the girls hobbled off the field when Coach Simmons called them over for a team announcement. Maddy kicked the ball around a few more times and then jogged over to where everyone was gathered. She noticed that the boys' team had also come over from their field to hear the announcement. They were huddled awkwardly alongside the girls' team.

"OK, everyone, quiet down. We have an exciting announcement. I'm going to let Josh Martin tell us the good news since he is the reason for it!" Coach Simmons said.

Maddy strained onto her tiptoes, trying to see over the crowd. Josh Martin had an announcement for *her* team?

Josh slowly stepped in front of Coach Simmons and cleared his throat. He tossed his hair out of his eyes and Maddy felt her stomach sink into her Adidases.

"I just wanted to let the girls' team know that I was able to work with Jessica Saunders, the student council president, this week to figure out a solution to your fund-raiser problem."

Maddy couldn't believe what she was hearing. *So that's why Josh was talking to Jessica so much!*

Josh continued a little more loudly, "Jessica has agreed to give forty percent of the money that is raised at tomorrow night's Valentine's Dance to the girls' soccer team to help them go to State this spring."

The girls let out a deafening cheer and started jumping up and down. They crowded around Josh to thank him and hear more about the details. Maddy stood frozen to her spot. She was totally speechless. And totally paralyzed. *Josh saved the fund-raiser*, she thought. *I can't believe it! Why did he do that? That was so nice of him!*

A million questions swirled in Maddy's mind as she stood at the back of the mob. Now she couldn't see Josh at all because of everyone surrounding him. They were all talking at once and laughing excitedly.

"Thanks again, Josh! You're an amazing team player," Maddy heard Coach Simmons say. She peered over the crowd to see Josh walking away with his teammates. They were patting him on the back and shoving him a little. The girls started moving off into smaller groups. Emma, Li, and Michele came running over to Maddy.

"Can you believe it!?" they shouted, grabbing Maddy's hands and jumping around in front of her.

Maddy still couldn't speak. *Did Josh do this for me?* she wondered, feeling even sicker once she realized he might like her, too. *What should I do? I should stop him and thank him, but I can't move!*

"Maddy? What's wrong with you?" Michele asked. She had the same worried look on her face that she'd had at lunch.

"I don't know what's wrong with me," Maddy blurted out. "I just can't believe it."

"I know. Josh is *sooo* sweet!" Li gushed.

"Did you ask him to do that?" Michele asked.

"What? No! I had nothing to do with it," Maddy responded. "He did it all on his own. . . ."

A huge grin spread across Michele's face. "That's amazing! He must really like you!"

Now a wash of crimson spread across Maddy's face. "I don't know. I mean, he just really likes soccer, I think. I don't think he likes me."

"Are you kidding?" Emma practically shouted. "Of course he does. There's no way a boy at Evergreen Middle School would do something like that for a girl if he didn't like her! I'm going to go ask Matt if he does!" Emma started to turn away toward the boys' field.

"NO!" Maddy grabbed her arm. "Please don't, Emma, I'll die!"

Seeing Maddy's panic-stricken face, she turned back. "OK, OK, I won't!"

"Are you sure you're alright?" Li asked. "Do you want to sit down?"

Maddy couldn't decide if she should tell her friends about her crush on Josh. She wanted to and figured they probably already knew since she was being such a freak, but it just didn't feel right to tell them before Sarah. She wanted Sarah's advice first, plus she didn't want anyone else on the team to hear her talking and go tell Josh. That would be a disaster!

"I'm OK, really," Maddy assured her friends. "I think my dad's waiting for me, so I guess I should go. I'll see you guys at school tomorrow! Bye!"

CHAPTER 10
The Phone Call

Maddy's dad talked about Josh the entire ride home from the gym. He seemed to be just as excited about Josh as Maddy was.

"That Josh Martin is such a good kid. He's a pretty smart boy, thinking up that scheme all on his own. Do you know him, Maddy? Josh Martin, I mean. What a nice boy."

Maddy kept quiet, not because she wanted to hear her dad talk about Josh, but because she was so deep in her own little world that she could barely hear him speaking.

As soon as Maddy opened the front door, Monica came bolting out of the kitchen.

"Maddy, you have to call Sarah right now. She's called like five times for you." Monica seemed half annoyed and half intrigued by Sarah's calls.

Maddy's entire face lit up. "Really? She has?"

"Yeah, you need a cell phone, Maddy."

"Tell that to Mom and Dad! I would *love* a cell phone!"

Just then the phone rang again. Maddy darted up the stairs as fast as she could.

"I'll get it in my room!" she shouted.

Maddy tore into her room, pushed the door hard with her foot, and dove onto the bed. She landed on her stomach as she grabbed for the phone.

"He . . . hello?" she answered as all the air left her stomach.

"Maddy?" Sarah's voice sounded a little hesitant.

"Sarah! I'm so glad to finally hear your voice!" Maddy blurted out. For a split second, she thought about trying to play it cool, but she couldn't help herself.

"Oh! I'm so relieved. You're not mad at me?" Sarah asked.

"Me, mad at you? Why would I be mad at you? I thought *you* were never going to speak to me again!"

"Well, I wasn't until Kyle called," Sarah squeaked into the phone.

"I'm so glad he called you! Did you say yes? Are you going to the dance?"

"Uh-huh!"

"Yay! I'm so excited for you, Sarah!"

"I couldn't believe when I answered my cell and it was Kyle! He told me about how he IM'ed you and that you told him the heart-o-gram was actually for Josh! Maddy, you have to tell me what happened!" Sarah said all at once.

"I know. We have so much to talk about! I don't even know where to begin." Maddy took a deep breath. "But first off, I want to tell you I'm sorry, Sarah. I'm sorry for being so hard to handle this past week. And I'm sorry I yelled at you for joining the decorating committee. And I'm sorry I didn't listen more when you didn't want to be involved in my anti-V-Day plan. And I'm sorry I've been so negative."

"I forgive you, Maddy. And I'm sorry, too. I wish I would have taken your soccer fund-raiser more seriously. I should have tried to think of a way to help."

"It's OK. It all worked out. But that's another story. I want to hear about Kyle's phone call!" Maddy knew Sarah was dying to tell her every detail.

"I really missed you, Maddy! This week was so weird. We missed our Monday IM update and Wednesday homework night. And not eating lunch or talking in English class was so hard!" Sarah went on.

"It was totally weird! I was so desperate to talk to you, especially yesterday and today. All I wanted to do was explain that the heart-o-gram wasn't for Kyle, but I couldn't find you anywhere! Where were you during English this morning, by the way?"

"Well . . . avoiding you, for one thing."

"I knew it!"

"But not just that. I wasn't finished designing the table centerpiece for the dance tomorrow night and Jessica wanted to see it at our lunch meeting to approve it. So my mom let me go to school late to get it done."

"OK. I guess that sounds legitimate enough," Maddy laughed.

"Maddy, I have to go help Jack set the table. Can you come over after dinner? I totally need your help planning an outfit for tomorrow night and I have to hear about the heart-o-gram for Josh!"

"You don't have your outfit planned yet?" Maddy was amazed. "I thought for sure you would have that and two back-ups ready the minute Kyle asked you."

"Nope. I need my BFF to help."

Maddy grinned. It was so good to hear Sarah call her BFF again. "I have to ask my parents, but I'm sure it will be fine. I think they're a little sick of me this week."

"Call me when you're done eating and let me know if you can come!"

"I will. I can't wait to catch up on everything!"

Maddy almost inhaled her dinner. She tried to cut her chicken so fast that the entire table was shaking.

"Maddy, calm down. I know you're excited to see Sarah but you're going to hurt yourself, or one of us!" Mrs. Wilkes cautioned.

"Yeah, Maddy, you better not fling gravy in my eye or something," Monica laughed, adding a dab of gravy to her forehead.

Maddy giggled back and stuck a piece of mashed potato to her nose.

"Well, looks like everything is back to normal." Mr. Wilkes shook his head. Then he took a string bean and put it under his nose like a mustache.

Maddy thought she was going to choke. She and Monica started laughing so hard tears were rolling down their cheeks. Mrs. Wilkes tried to keep a serious look on her face, but as soon as Mr. Wilkes joined in the laughter, she lost it, too. Soon the entire family was laughing hysterically and Pete was running in circles around the table barking his head off.

A few minutes later, Mrs. Wilkes wiped her eyes with her napkin. "Maddy, why don't you go to Sarah's before you and Monica start another round of hysterics? We'll take care of the dishes."

Maddy jumped up and knocked over her water glass, sending Monica into another fit of laughter. "Oops. Thanks, Mom, I'll just . . ."

"Go, Maddy! Quick, before you light something on fire!" Mr. Wilkes laughed, mopping up the water.

"OK, bye!"

Maddy felt nervous knocking on Sarah's front door. As soon as Jack flung the door open, though, and the warm glow of the living room and the familiar scent of vanilla that always seemed to permeate the Warren house hit her, she felt right at home again.

"Hey, Jack! Long time no see," she said, tussling his hair.

"Hey, knock it off!" He hated when Maddy did that. "Sarah!" he shouted at the top of his lungs.

Sarah and her mom emerged from the living room.

"Well, hello, Maddy. It's been awhile!" Sarah's mom said.

"Hi, Diane. Yes, it has!" Maddy always felt weird calling Sarah's mom by her first name, but she insisted.

"I bet you girls have a lot to catch up on. I'll bring up some cookies when they're done, OK?"

Sarah grabbed Maddy's arm and pulled her toward the stairs. "Thanks, Mom!"

"Yeah, thanks!" Maddy added.

Sarah opened her bedroom door and Maddy rushed in.

"Wow! What are you working on?" she exclaimed, holding up a piece of material from Sarah's sewing table.

"That's the skirt I was telling you about!" Sarah said proudly. "It's kind of like the one that girl with the long black hair made on that fashion design show on TV. I was hoping I'd have it finished in time for the dance, but working on the decorating committee took a lot more time than I thought it would!"

Maddy surveyed Sarah's room to make sure nothing had changed. Sarah loved switching the theme of her room and redecorating, but Maddy was relieved she hadn't made any changes this week. She still had the Asian theme she'd worked on a couple of months ago.

"So tell me about the decorating committee," Maddy asked, a little unsure if she was prepared to hear about Sarah's new friends.

Sarah flopped down on her bed and grabbed one of the red pillows. "It was so much fun, Maddy! I was totally the leader of the committee. I don't know how it happened, but I just had so many ideas and everyone was really into them!" she said all in a rush.

Maddy sat on the edge of Sarah's bed and pulled at a loose thread on the comforter. She didn't know why it felt weird to hear these things, but it did. Sarah could sense that Maddy was uncomfortable.

"It made me think about how much fun we've always had dressing up and coming up with different outfits. It made me wish you were on the committee, too. . . ." Sarah continued.

"I have always liked planning outfits and stuff, but I don't think I would have wanted to be on the decorating committee, Sarah," Maddy said matter-of-factly. "Do you think we just don't have enough of the same interests?" Maddy couldn't believe she'd actually asked that out loud. She'd been thinking it and worrying about it all week, but she wasn't sure she actually wanted to hear Sarah's response.

"I've been thinking about that, too," Sarah said quietly. A moment later, though, she slapped her hand onto the pillow. "But, Maddy, I missed you this week! I missed hearing about soccer and talking about your practice. Just because I don't play sports doesn't mean I don't like hearing about what you're interested in. And I missed telling you about my sewing project and about the decorations for the dance!"

Maddy's face brightened. "I missed you, too! Seeing you at that other lunch table was the weirdest thing ever. I was so worried you didn't want to be friends anymore."

"Honestly, I think I needed to see what it was like to hang out with different people," Sarah said. "You've always been the outgoing one and I've always been the quiet one. It felt good to be more of a leader and stuff."

"Sarah, I think that's great!" Maddy was truly happy for her. "I am so glad you were in charge of the decorating committee. I think you should start a design club or something!"

"Really?" Sarah beamed. "I love that idea! And Maddy, the other girls on the committee were so nice. I think you would really like them. And did you know that Nissa Long played soccer at her old school? She's dying to join your league — I have to introduce you!"

"That's awesome!" Maddy responded. It felt great to be hanging out at Sarah's again. She had been so worried all week that they weren't going to be friends anymore. But it seemed like their friendship was even stronger now that they both felt good talking about their own interests.

"I can't believe you've been here for over fifteen minutes and we haven't even talked about the heart-o-gram or Josh and Kyle!" Sarah pounded on her pillow.

"I know! OK, where to begin . . ." Maddy told Sarah the entire story about how Monica eavesdropped on her conversation with her mom and then acted weird the next morning before school. She explained how she saw the heart-o-gram on Josh's desk before class and that she was trying to find some place to hide it when she ran into Kyle. The girls laughed and Sarah covered her face, imagining how embarrassed Maddy must have been.

"I was *so* mad at you!" Sarah giggled. "I couldn't believe you were giving Kyle a heart-o-gram. I never really thought you had a crush on him, I just thought you were doing it to get back at me or something."

"No way!" Maddy exclaimed. "I was so mortified. All I wanted to do was hide under my desk for the next ten years!"

Maddy went on to give Sarah all the details of her IM chat with Kyle. Then she told her about how she had run into him on the way to soccer.

"So then I got this call on my cell phone!" Sarah interjected. "I didn't recognize the number, but I answered and it was him! He was so nervous! And the minute he said his name my stomach did like ten million flips!"

"Ugh! I hate that!" Maddy added.

"I know! So he was like . . . wait." Sarah stopped. "*You* hate that? Madeleine Wilkes. Do you have something to tell me?" Sarah started to smile.

Maddy's face got hot and red for the twentieth time that week. "Yes!" she cried into Sarah's comforter. "I have a crush on Josh Martin!"

Sarah jumped up from the bed and spun in a circle. "I knew it! I knew it!"

"Sarah, I've been dying to tell you! I don't know what to do! I need your help. And now he did this thing where he saved the soccer fund-raiser and I think he might have done it for me, but I'm not sure." Maddy struggled to catch her breath.

"What thing? What did he do?"

"I saw him talking to Jessica Saunders a couple of times this week. Can you imagine?"

"No way!" Sarah confirmed.

"I had no idea what they were talking about. I didn't even think they knew each other. And then I started to realize that I was jealous! I got so sick to my stomach, Sarah, when I finally understood that I really *did* have a crush on Josh!"

Sarah sat back down on the bed and pulled her legs up to her chest. She was so excited she could hardly contain herself.

"So then Josh wasn't in English class today, either. I couldn't believe it. I was kind of relieved, but I also really wanted to try to talk to him!"

"That's so weird — I wonder why he wasn't there."

"Well, I think I found out at soccer practice. After we were done, the coach called everyone over for an announcement, including the boys' team! And there was Josh. He told everyone that he had worked with Jessica to save our soccer fund-raiser."

"WHAT!?" Sarah was back on her feet.

"They're giving forty percent of the money raised at the Valentine's Day Dance to my soccer team!" Maddy was up now, too, and the girls were jumping up and down.

"Maddy, he totally did that for you! He likes you, I know he does!"

"Do you really think so?" Maddy asked, beside herself that she was finally talking about her crush with Sarah.

"There's no other explanation," Sarah said flatly. "Josh Martin likes you and he saved your soccer fundraiser to tell you that."

Maddy fell onto the bed on her stomach and kicked her legs. She'd never been so dramatic in her life, but she felt it was necessary given the circumstances.

"Maddy, you have to come to the dance with me!" Sarah cried. "Josh will be there. You guys can talk, he'll ask you to dance. It will be perfect!"

Maddy turned over and sat up, looking serious. "I don't know, Sarah. I've finally just come to terms with Valentine's Day. I don't know if I can actually go to the dance."

"You *have* to! How else are you going to get a chance to hang out with Josh?"

Sarah was right. There was never time to chat in English class. And soccer practice was hard, too — there were always so many people around.

"Well . . ." Maddy hesitated. "I guess maybe I could . . ."

"YAY!" Sarah screamed at the top of her lungs. "We're going to have the best time ever! Now we have to plan outfits for both of us."

"Oh, geez, you're totally right. I have *nothing* to wear!"

Sarah pulled every article of clothing she owned out of her closet and arranged it on her bed. She put skirts and pants on one side and shirts and sweaters on another. Then she arranged accessories on her sewing table.

"Let's start with you first," Maddy suggested. "I feel like you need first pick."

"OK," Sarah said, smiling. "So I was thinking about this . . . but tell me what you think." She held up a pair of gold shimmery tights and a black knee-length skirt with a ruffle at the bottom. "But I can't figure out what shirt to wear."

"I love those tights. They're perfect!" Maddy surveyed the pile of tops and held up a black button-down shirt. "What about this one? Too much black?" she asked, thinking of her own outfit from the day before.

"Yeah, probably," Sarah replied, throwing aside a few sweaters. "Oooo, maybe this one!" She held up a cream-colored short-sleeved sweater with flecks of sparkly gold thread in it.

"That's definitely it! Try it on."

Once Sarah had the tights, skirt, and sweater on, the girls picked out a pair of black shoes with a tiny heel and a buckle across the toe, long earrings made up of small intertwined gold hoops, a black bangle bracelet, and a delicate gold necklace with a little heart charm on it.

"You look amazing!" Maddy nodded her head in approval.

There was a quick knock on the door and Sarah went to open it.

"Here are your cookies, girls," Sarah's mom said in

a singsong voice. "Oh my gosh, Sarah, you look so . . . old!" she exclaimed, looking like she might cry.

"Really?" Sarah squealed as she ran over to her full-length mirror.

"You girls are growing up too fast. I can't stand it." Diane shook her head.

"Thanks for the cookies, Mom!"

"Yeah, thank you, Diane!"

"You're welcome. Maddy, don't stay too late, I don't want your mom to worry, OK?"

"OK."

Sarah ran back and closed the door. "OK, now it's your turn!"

"I don't know." Maddy was starting to have second thoughts. "You look so much older and I don't think I could wear an outfit like that. . . . Maybe I just shouldn't go."

"Maddy, don't be silly!" Sarah looked at her intently. "You don't have to wear something like this. You have your own style — we'll find something that you like, I promise."

"I guess I'll see what we find and then decide," Maddy offered.

"OK, let's get to work!"

First Sarah chose a pair of gray corduroy pants and a light pink top, but that didn't seem fun or fancy enough. Then Maddy tried on a black pencil skirt and a green button-up shirt, but that wasn't her style, either. She grabbed a notebook and pretended she was on a job interview. Sarah laughed and shook her head. "Next."

Then Sarah found a light blue denim skirt that hit just above the knee and had a tiny slit in the back. It fit Maddy perfectly. Next Maddy chose a light blue long-sleeved cotton shirt that made her eyes look great. Sarah held up a pair of tights that had light blue, dark blue, pink, yellow, and green stripes on them. They worked great with the outfit. Maddy chose a pair of small silver hoop earrings and a silver necklace with a tiny silver ring on it. It was perfect.

"The only thing is shoes . . . we're not the same size," Sarah pointed out.

Maddy sank down on the bed. She had forgotten about shoes. She was about to suggest a pair of Adidases when she remembered a pair of brown flats at the back of her closet.

"I can wear those brown leather flats my mom bought me at the beginning of the school year. I never wear them, and I think they're dressy enough," she suggested.

"Perfect," agreed Sarah.

Maddy stood up and moved in front of the mirror to see her outfit. She felt totally comfortable and looked great. "OK, I'll go."

CHAPTER 11
The Lunchroom

Friday morning was crisp and sunny, a little warmer than the rest of February had been in Hamilton. Maddy bounded out the front door of her house feeling like a different person. Being at Sarah's house again and talking through their fight made Maddy realize how important her friendship with Sarah was to her. She also felt a little older — a little more mature. She had worried so much about the idea that she and Sarah were growing apart: that they didn't have enough in common. But now she knew that their differences were what made them unique and what made them such great friends.

Maddy reached the park on Dogwood Avenue and Sarah was already there waiting. Maddy was surprised by how casually she was dressed. She was wearing a pair of brown Puma sneakers, dark jeans, and a brown T-shirt with a cream-colored cardigan sweater over it, paired with a black puffy coat with faux fur trim on the hood.

"I haven't seen you wear sneakers in a while," Maddy remarked.

"I know! I decided to dress casual today so Kyle will think I'm extra dressed up when he sees me tonight!" Sarah squeaked.

"Interesting plan," Maddy laughed.

"I'm so nervous about seeing him!" Sarah blurted out as they started walking toward Evergreen. "I didn't think I would be, but I totally am."

"I'm really nervous about seeing Josh, too. I haven't even thanked him for the fund-raiser thing yet." Maddy continued, "I was hoping he would be online last night when I got home from your house, but he wasn't. Though, I was kind of relieved, anyway."

The girls talked more about their outfits for the dance and their nerves about English class. They reached the school before they were fully prepared to see their crushes.

"Well, I guess we have no choice. We walked so

slowly I think we're almost late as it is," Sarah commented.

"Yep . . . here goes nothing,'" Maddy added.

Maddy thought that homeroom was at least five minutes shorter than usual. In no time she was headed into English class again. Sarah had already arrived and Kyle was leaning casually on her desk. *They look so comfortable and normal*, Maddy thought. Just then Kyle's elbow slipped off the desk and he practically fell out of his chair. He coughed nervously and tried to pretend nothing had happened. Sarah fidgeted and twirled a strand of hair around her finger, trying not to make eye contact with him. *OK, that's a little better*, Maddy chuckled to herself.

Maddy turned toward her spot and noticed that Josh wasn't in his. *Don't tell me he's not here again!* she worried. *What if he's still avoiding me? Sarah was wrong. He doesn't really like me!* Sarah and Maddy exchanged looks and Sarah shrugged. She didn't know where Josh was, either. Maddy took her seat as the final bell rang. She reached into her backpack on the floor and grabbed the book she had been reading. Mr. Anderson always gave them independent reading time on Fridays. She was hoping she could concentrate on her book and not on Josh. When she lifted her head, her stomach tightened into an even smaller knot. There was Josh. He slid into his seat right after the bell.

"That was a close one, Mr. Martin!" Mr. Anderson cautioned.

"Sorry," Josh mumbled.

Maddy leaned out in her chair hoping to get Josh's attention and at least say hi, but he was turned completely away.

"Alright, kiddies, it's independent reading time," said Mr. Anderson from his desk. "You've got twenty minutes to read whatever you want. Yes, even comic books, Kyle."

Maddy had an idea. She reached into her backpack and pulled out a piece of loose-leaf paper and a pen. She looked stealthily in Mr. Anderson's direction to see if he was reading, too. He was watching Maddy.

"Do you need something, Maddy?" he asked.

"No, Mr. A., I'm fine."

Maddy turned forward and hunched over in her chair. On the notebook paper she wrote:

Hi Josh. I didn't have a chance to thank you yesterday for the soccer fund-raiser. So thanks.

Maddy took a deep breath and continued writing.

Also, I was wondering if you're going to the dance tonight.

Her hand trembled as she folded the paper in half and then in half again. *Am I actually going to pass this to him? I have to!* Maddy steadied her hand and glanced quickly toward Mr. Anderson's desk. He was reading. Sarah looked up and mouthed, "What's going on?" Maddy nodded her head toward the note and Sarah smiled and nodded back in encouragement.

Maddy grabbed the note in her right hand and reached around Josh's side. She made sure to pass the note on the side that Mr. Anderson couldn't see from his desk. She tapped Josh's arm with the piece of paper. He moved his head toward it slightly and quickly grabbed the note.

Maddy thought she might pass out. She could hear him opening the paper, then silence while he read the note, then the sound of a pencil scratching out a reply. He passed the note back on the same side, down by Maddy's leg. She reached down and grabbed it quickly. *If Mr. A. sees us he's going to read it out loud! I know he will*, Maddy thought nervously. She opened the paper as quietly as she could and read:

No problem about the soccer thing.
And I was going to go to the dance, but the girl I like is going with someone else . . .

Maddy just stared at the paper. How could it be? Maybe Josh really *did* like Jessica. Maybe he used the soccer fund-raiser as an excuse to talk to her and ask her to the dance, but she already had a date! Maddy felt sick, but in a different way than she had been feeling. Now she felt crushed. Crushed by her crush! She crumpled up the paper as much as she could, not caring if Mr. Anderson caught her. Josh glanced back at Maddy. He seemed to be expecting a reply. Maddy stared hard right back.

"Maddy, this is reading time, not writing," she heard Mr. Anderson say. "Please put the paper away."

Maddy reached down and jammed the note into her backpack. She picked up her book and pretended to read. She could still feel Josh looking at her, but there was no way she was going to look up. If she did, she would cry.

At the second the bell rang at the end of the period, Maddy bolted from her chair even though Mr. Anderson was still talking. Sarah grabbed her arm as she flew by and Maddy mumbled, "I'll be in the bathroom."

By the time Sarah reached the bathroom Maddy was already crying full force in the last stall.

"Maddy, what happened?" Sarah asked, pulling the door open. "Are you OK?"

"No. I'm not OK," Maddy said between sobs. "Josh likes someone else."

"What? That's impossible!"

"No, it isn't. I asked him if he was going to the dance and he said the girl he wanted to ask is going with someone else!" Maddy cried, showing Sarah the note. "Do you think he means Jessica? I bet he does."

"No way. Jessica is going out with Devon Halverson. Everybody knows that."

"*I* didn't know that!" Maddy cried again.

"Calm down, Maddy. There has to be a perfectly good explan . . . wait a second!" Sarah's face lit up and she grabbed Maddy's hand. "Josh still thinks you like Kyle! He was standing right next to me on Wednesday when the whole heart-o-gram thing happened! I bet he just assumed you guys are going to the dance now because Kyle made a big deal of it in class." Sarah crossed her arms, satisfied with her realization.

Maddy tore off another wad of toilet paper and dabbed at her eyes. "Do you really think that's it?"

"There's no other explanation, Maddy. You have to go tell Josh what happened!"

Just then the first bell rang. Maddy ran to the sink and splashed water on her face. "I can't talk to him like this!" she exclaimed.

Sarah pulled a powder compact from her book bag. "Here, put some powder on your face — it will help conceal the red splotches."

Maddy stared down at the compact. "Are you wearing make-up now, Sarah? I meant to ask you last night. I thought I saw you wearing eye make-up in the cafeteria the other day and then I had this weird dream . . . well, never mind."

"Cassie, one of the eighth-graders at my lunch table, wanted to put a little mascara on me the other day, so I let her. My mom still won't let me wear mascara and eye shadow and stuff, but she bought me some powder and lip gloss."

"Good. I don't think I could handle it if you were wearing make-up every day now!"

Sarah laughed and started dotting powder over Maddy's cheeks.

"Find Josh after your math class! Your face will be fine by then."

"OK, I will. We're going to eat lunch together, right?" Maddy hesitated. She just remembered they'd had separate lunch groups all week.

"Oh, yeah." Sarah remembered, too. "Why don't we invite our tables to eat together?" she suggested.

"Good idea! OK, I'll find you in the caf after math," Maddy said as she grabbed her backpack.

"Good luck!"

Maddy ran down the hall as the final bell rang. She was late. She really hoped Ms. Jenkins would let it slide. She arrived at her classroom door to find that Ms. Jenkins wasn't even there. *That was a freebie!* Maddy thought as she noticed a substitute teacher frantically searching Ms. Jenkins's desk.

"Good morning, class. I'm Mr. Vanderhaus and I can't seem to find Ms. Jenkins's lesson plans. So, uh . . . since it's Friday and everything, why don't we just have a study period?"

The class cheered but the math period still crawled by. Maddy went over her speech to Josh at least forty-five times, which was about forty times too many. Now she was just a nervous bumbling mess about the whole thing. By the time the bell finally rang, she felt like she couldn't even remember her own name. She let her Jell-O legs carry her out into the hall and toward Josh's locker, but he wasn't there. Little did she know that Josh skipped his locker and went the long way to the cafeteria specifically to avoid seeing Maddy, but he did bump into Kyle and Glen.

"Hey, Josh," Kyle said, "I heard about that soccer fund-raiser thing. Nice job!"

"Oh, yeah, thanks," Josh mumbled.

"So, you going to the dance tonight?" Kyle asked.

"No . . . I assume you are, though?"

"Yeah, I'm going with Sarah Warren. I'm stoked."

Josh looked up and gave Kyle a weird look. "Sarah

Warren? I thought you were going with Maddy Wilkes."

"No . . . I asked Sarah."

"But Maddy gave you that heart-o-gram and everything. . . ."

"Oh, right, I forgot about that. No, dude, that was for *you*!" Kyle poked Josh in the chest for emphasis. "I talked to Maddy on IM and she said that the valentine was meant for you, which I was totally glad about because I wanted to ask Sarah to the dance," Kyle continued.

"It was for *me*?" Josh stared in disbelief and then put his hand to his forehead. "I just told Maddy I wasn't going to the dance because the girl I like is going with someone else. I thought she was going with you!"

"That sucks, dude," Kyle replied.

"Now what am I going to do?" Josh shook his head.

Glen moved in a little closer to Josh. "Hmmm . . . maybe I can help," he said.

After waiting at Josh's locker until her legs started to feel solid again, Maddy made her way to the cafeteria. She found Sarah seated at their favorite table with some of her decorating committee friends and the two eighth-grade girls Maddy had approached the day before. Maddy dropped her backpack at the table and then went to Li, Emma, and Michele's table to ask if they wanted to join. The girls grabbed their trays and followed Maddy to the new table.

Sarah and Maddy made all the introductions.

"Maddy, this is Nissa — the soccer player I was telling you about." Sarah motioned toward a tall, thin girl with cascades of dark red hair.

"Hey, Nissa, nice to meet you. We have a city league game at the indoor fields tomorrow morning; you should totally come and meet the coach and everything," Maddy suggested.

"Really? That would be awesome," responded Nissa.

"Sarah, you know Emma, Michele, and Li, right?" Maddy asked.

"Hey, guys, how are you?" Sarah smiled at them.

"I love your hair clip," Li commented.

"Thanks, I made it myself," Sarah replied. "I can show you how, it's super easy."

"I would love that!" said Li.

Maddy loved how easily their lunch tables were blending together. "Li, Sarah's going to start a design club — you should totally join."

"That's so cool." Li was impressed. "I would love to learn to sew or knit. My mom started to show me how to knit, but I got kind of bored. I'm sure that wouldn't happen in a design club, though!"

"It was Maddy's idea. Do you want to help me plan it?" Sarah asked.

"Totally!"

The girls started chatting and eating their lunches. They all had tons to talk about. Maddy made sure to sit next to Sarah so she could tell her that she hadn't spoken to Josh yet.

"I don't know what to do! I think he's avoiding me," Maddy whispered. She didn't want the whole table to get involved, not yet, anyway.

"Well he can't avoid you forever. We just have to find him. I'm sure he's just embarrassed or something," Sarah tried to reason.

All of a sudden, a piercing screech filled the lunchroom. Everyone covered their ears and gazed around the room. It sounded like the speaker system had been turned on. Maddy looked around, trying to figure out where the noise was coming from, and zeroed in on something awful: Glen Plimpton was standing near the hot lunch line positioning a microphone in a stand.

"Oh no! No way!" Maddy backed her chair away from the table and started to get up.

"Maddy, what is it?" Sarah asked as everyone at the table watched Maddy intently.

"This cannot be happening again. I can't stay here." Maddy shook her head and reached for her backpack. "Glen is about to embarrass me again! I have to get out of here." Maddy pulled hard on the strap of her backpack, not realizing that the zipper was open, and all of her books fell out on the floor. She dropped to her knees and frantically tried to stuff them back in the pack when she heard someone clear his throat into the microphone.

Maddy put her head in her hands and tried to crawl farther under the table. "Oh no! This is it!" she whimpered quietly, waiting for Glen's voice to squeal across the cafeteria.

"Um, sorry to, uh, bother everyone," she heard. It wasn't Glen's high-pitched, scratchy voice at all. It was a smooth, quiet voice — one that she recognized. It was Josh Martin's.

Sarah peeked under the table and grinned at Maddy. Maddy slowly started to crawl out and sat up on her knees, peering across the room.

"I just have something I wanted to ask someone and I couldn't seem to find her today. Um, Maddy Wilkes . . . I was wondering if you would, uh, go to the Valentine's Day Dance with me tonight?" Josh finished and stood still except for his right hand, which was twirling a drawing pencil in and out of his fingers, over and over again at light speed.

Before she even knew what was happening or even felt sure that Josh had actually said her name, Maddy stood up. By this time she and Josh were the only two people in the room that were standing. Maddy raised her hand and Josh looked in her direction, a small smile beginning to form on his face.

"Hi, Josh," Maddy said almost in a whisper.

"Louder!" shouted a boy from the eighth-grade corner, and several people laughed.

"Hi, Josh," Maddy tried again. "I would, um, love to go to the dance with you."

The entire lunchroom erupted into cheers and claps and whistles. Even the lunch ladies were clapping and smiling. Led by Sarah, Maddy's lunch table cheered the loudest.

CHAPTER 12

The Dance

That night Sarah's mom drove her to Maddy's house to get ready for the dance. Sarah brought both of their outfits and some other options, just in case either of them changed their minds at the last minute. Her mom agreed to let her wear a tiny bit of eye make-up, too, so she packed up a million little pots of color from her mom's make-up drawer.

The girls spent at least half an hour just trying on different eye shadow combinations before they settled on anything. They ran between Maddy's room and the bathroom to see their options in different lighting and at different angles. Monica was getting ready for the dance, too, and even asked Sarah and Maddy's advice on her outfit. She was wearing a long-sleeved black cotton wrap-around dress with a light pink cardigan over the top. She wore thin black tights and black pointy boots, kind of like Sarah's.

"Are you sure this looks OK?" she whined to Maddy and Sarah, turning in a circle for the tenth time. Of course, it looked perfect.

"Monica, you look fantastic!" Sarah gushed. "You totally look like a senior in high school."

Monica smiled at Sarah. That was just the kind of compliment she was hoping for. "Thanks. And that sweater is amazing, by the way," she added. "It looks so good on you."

Sarah beamed back. "Really? Thanks!"

Monica was even nicer to Maddy than usual. She felt like she still owed Maddy for convincing their parents to let her go to the dance. Plus, she hated to admit it, but she was pretty impressed that her little sister had finally managed to capture the attention of a boy who wasn't a total dork. Monica's kindness over the last couple of days hadn't gone unnoticed by Maddy, either. She was glad that Monica was being more civil to her. She knew it wouldn't last but she was enjoying it while it did.

"Maddy, you can borrow my charm bracelet if you want," Monica offered.

Maddy let her mouth drop open. "Wow, thanks, Monica!" she said, fastening the silver bracelet around her wrist.

"Just be careful with it. You know it's my favorite." Monica already seemed to be having second thoughts.

There was no way Maddy was giving up the chance to wear Monica's jewelry. "Don't worry, I will." She covered the bracelet with her hand.

"Is Dad driving you to the dance, too?" Maddy asked.

"No, Emily convinced her sister to take us. I'm *so* glad I don't have to be seen having Dad drop me off . . . I mean, no offense, but . . ."

"It's fine," Maddy mumbled.

"So who did you decide to go to the dance with, anyway, Monica?" Sarah asked, changing the subject. She wished they were getting a ride from a cool older sibling, too.

Monica leaned casually against the bathroom sink. "Well, I had *so* much trouble deciding whose invitation to accept — Daniel's or Conner's or Scott's or

Wilson's . . ." Sarah and Maddy's eyes got wider with every name that Monica listed.

"So, I just decided to go in a big group of friends. I think it will be more fun that way, anyway!" Monica shrugged like it was no big deal.

Maddy hated to admit it, but she was a tiny bit impressed that Monica had chosen her friends over a boy. She always thought of her as so boy-crazy, but she was glad to see Monica put her friends first.

"I mean, I could have probably convinced all those boys to take me, but . . ." Monica laughed, throwing her head back.

Maddy laughed, too. *I guess she hasn't changed all that much*, she thought.

"Girls!" Maddy's mom called up the stairs. "We want to get some pictures of you before you go. Are you almost ready?"

"We'll be down in a sec, Mom," Maddy answered.

The girls took one last turn in front of the full-length mirror in Maddy's room and then grabbed their coats and bags and hurried downstairs. Monica was already in full glamour-shot mode in the living room. Maddy rolled her eyes at Sarah and she giggled.

"OK, where do you want us?" Maddy asked her dad, who was struggling to keep up with all of Monica's poses.

"Let's get a few of all three of you girls by the fireplace," he suggested.

The girls stood side by side, trying to remember to stand up straight and not blink as the flash hit their eyes. Sarah's mom took a couple of pictures and then Maddy's dad took a few more.

Mrs. Wilkes stood off to the side with her hands clasped in front of her chest. "You girls just look wonderful," she cried.

Just then Pete tore into the room with Jack running after him. Jack had been throwing the ball for Pete in the backyard. The girls practically jumped into the fireplace to avoid getting dog hair or slobber on their outfits. Mr. Wilkes grabbed Pete by his rhinestone collar and made him sit. Once he had calmed down,

Maddy decided he should be in one of the pictures, so the girls posed with Pete and Jack, too.

A few minutes later the doorbell rang and Monica ran to answer it. They could hear her squealing and stomping around in her boots.

"It must be Emily." Maddy rolled her eyes again.

Monica and Emily strutted into the living room. Emily was wearing skinny jeans tucked into knee-length boots and a flowing floral print shirt cinched up with a big belt at her waist. She had huge gold hoop earrings on and more eye make-up than Maddy, Sarah, and Monica combined. Maddy's parents looked a little nervous.

"Uh, hi, Emily. Don't you look nice," Mrs. Wilkes said.

"Hiya, Mrs. W!" Emily shouted. She was so ready to be a cheerleader at Hamilton High next year that practically everything she said came out as a cheer.

"Dad, can you get a couple of pics of me and Em real quick? Her sister is waiting in the car."

"Sure, yeah, alright," Mr. Wilkes stammered, still looking a little uneasy.

The girls struck a few dramatic poses and Mr. Wilkes again struggled to keep up.

Monica grabbed the camera from her dad to review the shots with Emily. "Perfect!" she announced.

"Thanks, Mr. W!" Emily barked.

"Alright, girls, please be careful. And Emily, tell your sister that Monica needs to be home by eleven. No excuses."

"No problem!" Emily cheered again.

"Bye-eee!" Monica called out as she and Emily clomped down the hall.

As soon as the door closed, Maddy's parents and Sarah's mom all let out a huge breath and then started laughing. Maddy and Sarah giggled, too, though they weren't sure if their parents were laughing at the same thing they were.

"Alright, girls, are you ready?" Mr. Wilkes asked. Maddy and Sarah were meeting Josh and Kyle at the front of the school.

"We're ready," they said together, gathering their things.

"Have fun, girls. And Maddy, be sure to meet your dad at the front of the school as soon as the dance is over. Got it?" Maddy's mom called after them, holding Pete's collar so he wouldn't beg to ride along.

"Yes, have a great time, girls." Sarah's mom waved with one hand while holding on to Jack's arm with the other so he wouldn't beg to ride along, either.

The girls sat in the back seat of Mrs. Wilkes's car and giggled excitedly.

"I can't believe this!" Maddy whispered, grabbing Sarah's hand. "I'm really glad you convinced me to come to the dance tonight — even before Josh asked me in front of the entire school!"

"Me, too, Maddy! It wouldn't have been the same without my BFF!"

Sarah gave Maddy a sly smile. "So, are you ready to admit that Valentine's Day isn't so bad after all?"

Maddy smiled back. "I suppose it could have been worse," she responded. "OK, a lot worse!"

Sarah laughed.

They pulled up to the school and saw Josh and Kyle sitting on the front steps waiting for them.

"Thanks, Dad!"

"Thanks, Mr. Wilkes."

"OK, girls, have fun. See you at eleven." Mr. Wilkes slowly pulled away from the curb as Josh and Kyle stood up from the steps.

"Are you ready?" Sarah squeezed Maddy's hand.

"I guess so!" Maddy answered.

Maddy opened the top of her bag and showed it to Sarah. Sitting next to her wallet and her lip gloss was her newest pair of Adidas. Sarah put her hands on her hips.

"Just in case . . ." Maddy argued, pointing out the brand-new pink laces she had added in honor of V-Day.

Sarah shook her head and gave Maddy a huge grin. "Come on, let's go!"